# WATCHING AND WRITHING

Fargo cursed his feeling of utter helplessness, but he knew he had to wait. There were too many Cheyenne for him to take on before the time was right. He had to wait—and watch what was happening.

He saw the six captured white women stripped naked by the braves. Then one redskin stepped forward. There could be no doubt who this towering, superbly muscled figure was. *Night Claw*.

The Cheyenne chief pointed at one of the women, a dark-haired girl with a full figure and heavy breasts. Two braves seized her by the arms and held her. Night Claw stepped forward and she screamed.

Fargo wanted to turn his eyes away, but he couldn't. The savage orgy of relentless rape and brutal murder was only just beginning—and he had to find a way to bring it to an end with flaming lead, cold steel, or just his white-knuckled bare hands. . . .

# SAVAGE GUNS

# THE TRAILSMAN

## 150

# SAVAGE GUNS

by

## Jon Sharpe

A SIGNET BOOK

SIGNET
Published by the Penguin Group
Penguin Books USA Inc., 375 Hudson Street,
New York, New York 10014, U.S.A.
Penguin Books Ltd, 27 Wrights Lane,
London W8 5TZ, England
Penguin Books Australia Ltd, Ringwood,
Victoria, Australia
Penguin Books Canada Ltd, 10 Alcorn Avenue,
Toronto, Ontario, Canada M4V 3B2
Penguin Books (N.Z.) Ltd, 182–190 Wairau Road,
Auckland 10, New Zealand

Penguin Books Ltd, Registered Offices:
Harmondsworth, Middlesex, England

First published by Signet, an imprint of Dutton Signet,
a division of Penguin Books USA Inc.

First Printing, June, 1994
10  9  8  7  6  5  4  3  2  1

The first chapter of this book originally appeared in *Springfield Sharpshooters*, the
one hundred forty-ninth volume of this series.

 REGISTERED TRADEMARK—MARCA REGISTRADA

Printed in the United States of America

# The Trailsman

Beginnings . . . they bend the tree and they mark the man. Skye Fargo was born when he was eighteen. Terror was his midwife, vengeance his first cry. Killing spawned Skye Fargo, ruthless, cold-blooded murder. Out of the acrid smoke of gunpowder still hanging in the air, he rose, cried out a promise never forgotten.

The Trailsman they began to call him all across the West: searcher, scout, hunter, the man who could see where others only looked, his skills for hire but not his soul, the man who lived each day to the fullest, yet trailed each tomorrow. Skye Fargo, the Trailsman, the seeker who could take the wildness of a land and the wanting of a woman and make them his own.

*1860, north of Medicine Bow,*
*where the Wyoming and Colorado Territories*
*meet and savagery proves it can*
*wear many faces . . . .*

# 1

The Indian rode out of the line of hackberry just as the small squad of blue-uniformed soldiers came along. Near naked, wearing only a pair of tattered and abbreviated britches, his muscular, bronze body burnished in the sun, he crossed in front of the eight troopers, wheeled his pinto, and put the horse into a gallop. "After him," the sergeant at the head of the squad hissed. "Let's find out what he'd doing around here." He snapped the reins over his brown army mount and the troopers gave chase. The Indian's thick, bear-greased hair hung almost to his shoulders and flew from side to side as he raced his pinto across a low rise.

He glanced back and saw the sergeant and his men riding full out. Snapping his knees into the sides of the pinto, he felt the horse respond at once, immediately lengthening its smooth stride to stay a dozen yards ahead of the pursuing soldiers. The land suddenly turned open, low brush and rock formations fronted by scraggly hawthorns. The Indian managed to keep his distance ahead of his pursuers when he spotted the opening between two high granite formations. He swerved and sent the pinto racing through the narrow opening, glanced back again, and saw the sergeant follow at once. The opening broadened into a long cut with hawthorn lining both sides, and the Indian raced the pinto down the center. The squad of troopers were still a dozen yards behind him and the cut narrowed, becoming almost a bottleneck of land.

The Indian kept at a gallop through the narrow neck of land and had just passed through when he saw the high wall of stone rise up in front of him. He rode to the wall and turned to face his pursuers. On each side of him was a line of scrubby, twisted hawthorns and behind them the high walls of rock.

"We've got him," the sergeant exulted as he raced through the bottleneck. "It's a damn box canyon." He was only a few yards from the Indian when out of the corner of his eye he caught the flicker of movement to his left, then another to his right. He reined up short and the men following him almost crashed into him as they pulled back on their mounts. "Shit," the sergeant bit out as he saw the dozen figures step from the hawthorns on both sides of him, drawn arrows on each bow. He heard the murmur of dismay from the troopers behind him. He swore again, bitterly this time as he realized they were entrapped. A hail of arrows would cut them down before they had a chance to bring carbines up.

The lone brave they had chased moved his horse toward them at a slow walk. Less than a yard away, he swung long legs over the pinto's back and dropped to the ground. Reaching up with one hand, he took hold of his thick, greased hair and with a sudden yank pulled it off. A shock of black, tousled hair sprang up underneath and the sergeant swallowed hard as he stared at the Indian's lake-blue eyes. "Jesus, you're the general's man," he said. "You're Fargo. He told us you'd show up anytime, anywhere."

"Bull's-eye," the tall, muscled man said as he watched the sergeant exchange pained, sheepish glances with his squad. "These are some old friends," Fargo said, gesturing with a wave of his arm to the Indians surrounding the squad. "They're members of the Arikara." He turned, spoke to the Indians in the Caddoan tongue which they shared with the Pawnee and the Wichita. The Indians lowered their bows, stepped back into the hawthorns, and emerged on their ponies to ride slowly away. Fargo returned his eyes to the small squad of troopers and the sergeant pushed his hat back on his head.

"It seems we really screwed up," he admitted.

"You did, but that's not important. The important thing is why and do you know what you did wrong," Fargo said.

"I didn't think we did anything wrong. We saw a damn Indian and we wanted to question him. He ran and we chased him," the sergeant said.

"No, you didn't just see him. First error. He rode out in front of you. He crossed your path. He deliberately let you see him. You should have realized that something was wrong right then," Fargo said. "Then he led you on a chase and rode into a box canyon where he was trapped. All you saw was that it was a box canyon and you had him but you should've known better. That should have sent a signal to you."

"We figured he'd made a mistake," one of the men said.

"An Indian wouldn't make that kind of mistake. Here's a man who knows this territory the way you know your barracks. He knows every damn inch of it, every stand of timber, every rock, every trail, every cut, and every arroyo. Suddenly he rides into a box canyon and traps himself?"

The sergeant exchanged sheepish glances with the others and blew a deep breath of air from his lungs. "Lesson number one, I'd say," he admitted.

"You thought you were chasing but he was leading. You know that old saying, look before you leap? Well, think before you chase, especially Indians. That's it for today," Fargo said.

"Thanks," the sergeant said and the others murmured

agreement. "The general warned us the lessons would come when we didn't expect them. You're working with Davis and three others from Squad Two, I hear."

"Right. See you around," Fargo said and the sergeant saluted as he led his men out of the small canyon. They'd remember the lesson, Fargo knew. Object lessons were the kind you remembered, especially when they realized they'd be dead if it hadn't been a lesson. He pulled himself onto the Ovaro and slowly rode from the canyon, turned right, and finally halted beside a small hill pond. He pulled the tattered britches off and, naked, slid his beautifully muscled frame into the water. He let himself float in the warmth of the sun and the cool of the pond before he began to rub the dye from his skin. He had used juniper berries mixed with agrimony to achieve the bronzed color and he watched the dye slowly wash from him in the water. Finally he swam to shore and drew himself onto a bank of soft elf-cap moss, where he stretched out and let the sun dry his nakedness.

This was rich land, between the Roan Plateau and the mountains of the Park Range, themselves a part of the southern end of the Rocky Mountains' vast range down through the Colorado Territory. But he wasn't here to vacation, of course, and he let himself turn thoughts backward to the message from General Miles Stanford, a summons more than a message. He had worked with Miles Stanford before, and they still owed each other favors above and beyond the call of duty. Or money, Fargo smiled. "Need you and your special talents," the message had read. "Double usual army fee." He had just finished a job in the Utah Territory and decided seeing the general again would be in order. Besides, in his quiet wisdom Miles had included an added incentive. "Monica Daly is here, working at the trading store," he had said and a rush of old memories had erupted at once, all of them good. Monica had been a hired bookkeeper when Miles commanded Fort Dodge and found he had a quartermaster who knew nothing about keeping records.

Monica had been memorable in a lot of ways, Fargo recalled, mostly because she had understood him better than most women did and had cheerfully accepted the facts of his world. Now the general and Monica were at Camp Campbell, which was not a major line fort like Dodge, yet it was entrusted with keeping the peace over a huge and sprawling area that extended into Utah. A stockaded camp, it hovered over a number of stores and trading posts as well as the small village of Campbell that lay practically in its shadow. When he had arrived, General Stanford had immediately sat down with him over a decanter of good bourbon. "I've a lot of young troopers here. Many will stay here but some will be transferred to other posts. You know the ways of the army. I want the best of them to become an elite corps. I want my men to be able to work without depending on Indian scouts for hire," the general had said. "I want them to learn how to become good trackers on their own and I want them to learn the ways of the Indian so they can keep their scalps wherever they may be sent. I don't expect you to make them into trailsmen but you can teach them a lot."

"It's not what I expected, Miles," Fargo had answered. "But you're paying double and it might be fun."

"I've told the men I want trained that I've sent for someone who'll teach them what I want them to know. I'll give you the names of the men and the squads. The rest is up to you. Do it in any way you think best."

They had spent the rest of the afternoon going over the exact things Miles wanted his men to learn and when evening drifted down, Fargo rose to his feet and drained the last up of his bourbon. "You said Monica was here," he remarked and the general let a sly smile touch his face.

"I wondered how long you'd take to get around to that," Miles said.

"I was on my best behavior," Fargo said. "Did you tell her I was coming?"

"Thought you'd like surprising her," General Stanford said and that's how it was done. The trading post was one of the structures in the shadow of the stockade and Monica lived at the rear. Fargo's smile widened as he thought about that night. Surprises can bring special rewards and Monica's surprise had been total, his reward more than worth the trip. Now, as he lay under the sun, he was glad he'd answered the general's summons, not only because of Monica but because he was enjoying teaching the young troopers things that could save their lives or advance their careers. He sat up, finally, his body dry and warm, and he rose and retrieved his clothes, Colt, and saddle from where he had hidden them. Dressed, he saddled the Ovaro and made his way back to the stockade where the three young troopers were waiting. They mounted their red-brown army horses and were about to ride off with him when the general hurried from his quarters.

"Got a real lead for you," he said. "Sid Burrows just left here, less than an hour ago. Sid has a hog farm and he cures and sells his aged hams. An Indian stole one of his best hams from the barn, third time in two weeks. It'll be a fairly fresh trail."

"Let's go," Fargo said and the three troopers swung alongside him. The troopers knew the location of the Burrows place and led the way. They reached the farm in ten minutes at a fast canter and Burrows came out at once.

"He was on foot," he said. "That's how bold they're getting. You find the bastard."

Fargo, staying atop the Ovaro, had already picked up the Indian's footprints and motioned to the three troopers to follow. "He headed for that stand of timber," Fargo said.

"He was pretty damn bold to come on foot," Trooper Davis said.

"Smart, not bold. There's little cover around the Burrows place. He could get closer on foot," Fargo said.

"But lugging a whole hamhock for God knows how far?"

"I'd guess he had a horse waiting in that timber," Fargo said as they reached the trees, mostly box elder and black oak, and he slowly moved the Ovaro into the forest. He halted some fifty yards into the timber and pointed to the hoofprints on the ground, pressed clearly into soft forest soil. "There's where he had his horse," Fargo grunted and the troopers followed as he moved forward. The prints were easy enough to follow until the soil grew firmer, and suddenly they vanished as the ground became layered with small, flat stones. Fargo glanced at the soldiers and saw their exchange of baffled frowns. "He didn't disappear," Fargo smiled.

"He just could have gone in any direction," one of the men grunted.

Fargo paused before answering, his eyes slowly scanning the ground that stretched ahead of them. "That way," Fargo said, pointing between two oaks.

"How do you know?" Trooper Davis said.

"You lose your trail on the ground, you look for it someplace else. It'll be there," Fargo said. "Look at those young branches low on the trees. The leaves are still brushed back, some of the ends broken. That's from a horse pushing past them. He also got off his horse to make it lighter and make sure no prints showed. He dismounted right here."

"How the hell do you know that?" another of the young troopers said, awe in his voice.

"He was sloppy, probably hurrying. See those flat stones right there. They've been kicked aside, a half-dozen of them. That's where he dismounted and shuffled his feet, probably trying to keep hold of the hamhock," Fargo said and led the way on, following the path of the snapped twigs and brushed leaves. He halted another twenty yards on and pointed to the forest floor, where a pair of carrion beetles and a tumblebug were flattened on the ground. A few feet further a dozen carpenter ants were crushed. "There's another sign you can use when hoofprints disappear," he told his pupils. "Insects crushed into the ground. Something heavy came down on them."

"Such as a hoof," Davis said.

"Bull's eye." Fargo smiled and moved forward. The nature of the forest floor changed a few hundred yards on, reverting to its soft, leafy underpinnings, and the hoofprints became clear again. Another hundred yards and Fargo drew up to a swift-running, fairly deep brook. He waited and watched the three troopers peer across the brook to the other shore.

"No hoofprints," Davis said. "Damn, he's smart. He went into the brook. Now we've really lost him."

"He's smart. He expected to be chased, but maybe we haven't lost him," Fargo said.

"He could've gone upstream or down. It'd be a pure guess on our part," Davis said and fell silent as he followed Fargo's eyes as they scanned the sides of the stream.

"He went upstream," Fargo said, moving the Ovaro up to its ankles in the water.

"You're not guessing. I know better than that," the trooper said.

"You want to trail someone, you have to look at the little things, the things that seem unimportant, the things easy to miss. This stream is running fairly flat and fast. Little sprays of water are tossed up onto the banks. But when I move my horse through it there's more water tossed up high on the banks," Fargo said. "Look at the watermarks downstream and the one upstream."

"The ones upstream are higher on the banks," Trooper Davis said. "Not much but definitely higher."

"Because he went upstream and the water hit against his horse's ankles and flew higher up on the banks," Fargo said. "Fall in behind me single file." The soldiers followed with murmured expressions of awe as he moved the Ovaro through the center of the stream, his eyes flicking from bank to bank. Finally he halted and gestured to where the hoofprints led onto the bank from the stream. "He's getting sloppy. He probably figures he's lost anybody chasing after him by now," Fargo said and sent the pinto onto the shore. He followed the line of hoofprints for another few thousand yards and reined to a halt. "We're not the only ones trailing him," he said, motioning to the set of pawprints that had suddenly appeared.

"Wolf?" one of the soldiers said tentatively and Fargo nodded.

"Got wind of the hamhock and decided to follow his nose," Fargo said. "This makes it easier for us. We follow the follower. He won't be hiding his trail."

"I thought wolves hunted in packs," one of the soldiers remarked as Fargo steered the pinto after the pawprints.

"Usually but not always. It depends to some extent on the kind of prey they're chasing," Fargo explained. "A big male like this will often go off in his own."

"How do you know it's a male?" Davis frowned and Fargo slowed to point to a tree as they passed.

"Look at the base of that tree. He stopped to pee on it. He's marking his territory. That's the third tree I've seen marked. It's what the male wolf does, mark his territory," Fargo said and rode on, putting the horse into a canter. The trees began to thin out as the forest came to an end and he slowed to a walk. The last of the box elder rose in front of him and the land sloped downward, dotted with tall, thick brush. At the bottom of the slope a fallen tree stretched across the ground and Fargo saw the Indian there, seated and using his knife to cut pieces of the hamhock for himself. Fargo whispered to the troopers. "You circle right and left. I'll go straight down," he said and waited for thirty seconds as the soldiers began to move out of the trees. They were going down the slope to form a pincer when he sent the Ovaro downward at a gallop.

The Indian leaped to his feet at the sudden sound, whirled, surprise on his face, a piece of still-unchewed ham hanging from the side of his mouth. He dropped the stolen meat as he spun again and leaped onto his horse to flee. But the troopers were at the bottom of the slope, closing off both sides, and Fargo raced downward. The Indian, clothed in a pair of leather leggings, tried to run but Trooper Davis cut him off and the other two soldiers were atop him before he could turn their way. He sent his pony leaping across the fallen tree trunk, only to find Fargo racing at him.

A young buck, he was not about to surrender easily, and he veered his pony to the right as Fargo reached him and tried to race past the Ovaro. Fargo dived from the saddle, closed both arms around the Indian, and fell with him to the ground. He landed on top and heard the breath rush from the red man with a hard gasp. The three troopers arrived as Fargo rose and pulled the Indian to his feet. "We'll take him," Davis said. "We'll bring him back and let the general decide what to do with him." Fargo nodded just as he glimpsed the gray form streaking across the ground, the hamhock in its mouth. He watched the wolf disappear into the trees and smiled. "That's called making the most of your opportunities," he said and Trooper Davis tied the prisoner and set him on his pony.

"Let's get back," he said.

"You got him. Successful mission," Fargo said.

"It wouldn't have been except for you," Davis said.

"You'll do it on your own next time," Fargo said.

"We just might," the trooper smiled. "We'll be remembering everything you taught us." He put his mount into a canter and Fargo rode along as they returned to Camp Campbell, where he stopped in at the general's quarters.

"You wondering what I'll do with that Indian thief?" the general asked and Fargo nodded. "Probably hold him a week and then let him go. He's a thief, nothing more, and he'll have learned a lesson he can carry back to his tribe. He's a Ute and they don't give us much trouble. I'm harsh when harshness is required and reasonable when reasonableness is right. Keeping things peaceful is a kind of balancing act."

Fargo nodded agreement. It was the kind of wisdom he expected from Miles Stanford and was all too seldom found in other places.

When darkness descended he found himself in Monica's bedroom, her softness surrounding him. Dark-haired, with a pleasant face, Monica was all roundness that somehow avoided being plump. She had a round, compact figure, round shoulders, hips rounded, breasts high and standing out almost straight. Monica's emotions seemed to echo her physical contours, all enveloping sweet softness, her lovemaking a thing of tempered earthiness, her soft thighs pressing hard around him, and her convex little belly quivering as she rose and fell with him. She held his face to her breasts, almost smotheringly, yet with a gentle tenderness. Even at that culminating peak of pleasure when she climaxed with him and emitted low, throaty groans, there was more simple, grateful satisfaction than wildness. She was not without passion but it was a gentle passion that brought its own kind of pleasure and after they finished he always had the consuming desire to caress her rounded body. Perhaps because she invoked the need for caring instead of just screwing. It had always been that way with Monica and it was still that way, he had found out.

He lay beside her, his hand idly stroking her round little

19

belly, moving up to circle the full, round breasts that jutted out from her. "How long will you stay on, Fargo?" he heard her ask.

"A while, I'd guess. Miles wants me to teach them all I can while I'm here," he told her and she almost purred in satisfaction.

"Good," she said and pulled his face against her breasts. "Teach them slowly." He went to sleep with his lips pressed against one round breast and when morning came the bugle woke him and he washed and dressed as Monica made coffee. Outside, four troopers from Squad 3 were waiting for him and Miles came from his quarters with his face set.

"Trouble?" Fargo queried.

"Not yet but that ham thief you caught yesterday turns out to be a favorite nephew of a chief just across the Utah Territory line," the general said.

"You going to let him go and head off problems?" Fargo inquired.

"No, that'd be a sign of weakness and cause more trouble down the line. I'm going to hang tough and let him go when I'm ready. But that means we'll have to prepare for anything the chief might decide to do. Maybe he'll just threaten and blow off steam. Maybe he'll try to test me. There's no way of knowing right now. Meanwhile, you be careful. I'm going to be working out a schedule for extra patrols."

Fargo nodded and rode away from the stockade with the troopers and spent the day teaching them how to cover their own trails, when to be careful about taking cover in woods and how to spot false trails left to send them in the wrong direction. He saw no sign of any increased Indian activity and the day was drawing to a close when he returned to the camp to find the general looking unhappier than when he'd left. "More bad news?" Fargo asked.

"Yes. Not in my backyard but still close enough," General Stanford said. "I'm glad you're here, Fargo."

"Me?"

"You know the Wyoming Territory. I remember you had Indian contacts there," the general said.

"A few. What's this all about?"

"I'm changing your assignment," Stanford said. "You'll be going north, into the Wyoming Territory east on Medicine Bow. I've already written a letter stating that you're representing me."

Fargo's brows lifted. "To do what?"

"Report back to me with facts. Find out what's going on," the general said. "A courier came in a few hours ago with news that there's real trouble up in Wyoming. It seems a powerful chief has decided to hit the warpath. I want to know if there's any special reason and what's being done."

"By whom?"

"By General Wendell Carter."

"You have a force up there?"

"At Camp North Platte, right by the river, and that's what's really making me nervous."

"I'm not following you," Fargo said.

"General Wendell Carter is a damn misfit. He became a general through connections in Washington and he has no business heading a regiment up in that territory. But he's there and if he messes up it can spread like wildfire. He's a brigadier general and as a major general I outrank him. But to get him removed I'll have to go through channels and you know how goddamn long that could take," Miles Stanford said bitterly.

"Red tape on top of red tape." Fargo nodded.

"Meanwhile, all hell breaks loose here. I want you to get up there and find out what's going on and head off anything you can. If you can't stop anything, come back and report to me. Maybe things will have calmed down enough here by then so I can leave and pay Carter a visit myself. You'll leave in the morning."

"You're changing our agreement, Miles," Fargo said.

"And adding a bonus," the general snapped.

"Fair enough," Fargo smiled.

"You still drive a hard bargain, don't you?" Stanford growled.

"You're still stingy with the army's money," Fargo laughed as he exited from the room. He hurried to Monica.

"Damn," Monica said. "I knew it was too good to last."

"I expect to be back," he told her.

"And I know better than to expect anything where you're concerned," Monica grumbled, but her arms came up to encircle his neck. "But I know you'd rather stay and that makes me feel good." She fell back onto the bed with him and proceeded to turn disappointment into desire, petulance into passion. When morning came she clung a little tighter and he held her a little longer. But finally he made his way to General Stanford's office, where he walked in through the open door and came to a halt.

The general stood behind his desk, facing a young woman who wore a deep-purple traveling jacket and skirt with a white blouse. Fargo found himself staring at hair the color of sun-dried wheat that hung shoulder length around a face of almost perfect features. She had a thin, straight nose, high-planed cheekbones, sharply etched lips, blue-gray eyes, and eyebrows that arched as they matched the sun-dried wheat hair. Tall, with long lines and a bustline he couldn't really see under the jacket, her utter loveliness was marred by a cool, almost disdainful haughtiness as she looked at him.

"Sorry, I'll come back," Fargo said to Miles.

"No, stay. This young lady just arrived on the early stage that stops by weekly, more or less," the general said. "She wants me to furnish her with a military escort to go on north."

Fargo watched the young woman turn an icy stare at the

22

general. "I think I've every right to expect no less, General," she said, words beautifully clipped, the result of fancy schools.

"What you expect and what I can do are two different things, young woman," General Stanford said, glancing at Fargo again. "This is Miss Alison Carter, Fargo," he said. "She's General Carter's daughter." Fargo felt his own brows arch. "This is Skye Fargo, Miss Carter," the general said. "He works on special assignments for me."

Fargo saw Alison Carter pause to go over the chiseled strength of his face before allowing a deprecating nod. "How nice," she said, dismissal in her tone, and turned back to the general. "I've a letter in my purse from the Secretary of the Army in Washington asking that I be given cooperation, and I still haven't heard a reason why you can't afford me an escort," she said.

"I can't give you an escort because I can't spare two troopers, much less an escort, to take you anywhere, and I don't give a damn how many letters you have in your purse," the general snapped and glared at Alison Carter. She kept her cool haughtiness, Fargo noted. "Does your father know you're coming to see him?" Miles questioned her.

"No," Alison Carter said, hesitating a half-second.

"I can tell you he's not going to want you visiting him now," the general said.

"I can't wait for him to want a visit from me. I've come on an important family matter," Alison said. "And I can't go on alone. I'd be lost before the first day was over."

"As well as scalped," Stanford grunted. "I've one thing I can do. Fargo, here, is on his way to pay a visit to your father. You can go with him."

She shot a frown at Fargo. "One man?" she protested.

"You'll have a better chance getting there with this one man than a squad of my troopers," the general told her.

23

"Cut the flattery," Fargo interrupted. "We have to have a talk."

"Would you excuse us a moment, Miss Carter?" the general said and, her smooth brow furrowed with an annoyed frown, Alison Carter strode from the room.

"This wasn't part of our bargain," Fargo hissed at Miles Stanford. "Things are simmering here and God knows what I'll find when I reach the Wyoming Territory. Getting through alone will be tough enough."

"You can do it if anyone can. Besides, this may be a great way to get on Carter's good side. He'll be real grateful to you for having brought his daughter through safely," the general said. "It could make him real cooperative."

"And what if I don't get her there?" Fargo questioned.

"You don't mention her. You just carry on with my instructions."

Fargo stared at the general. "You old son of a bitch," he breathed.

Miles Stanford didn't blink. "I have to find out what's going on up there. That comes before misfit generals and headstrong daughters," he said. "Take her along and I'll owe you one." Fargo grimaced but made no reply and the general called out to the young woman. "Please come in, Miss Carter," he said. Fargo watched Alison Carter return, the cool disdain in her blue-gray eyes. "Fargo will take you with him," the general said.

She turned her eyes on Fargo. "Am I to consider this some sort of grand favor?" she asked.

"You're damn right," Fargo growled. "And not one I'm happy about."

"That makes two of us," she sniffed and shot the general an icy glance. "This hardly fits my definition of cooperation," she said.

"That's too bad but it's the best I can do," Miles Stanford said calmly and Fargo moved to the door and paused.

"You coming?" he tossed back at her and she stepped toward him and caught up to him outside. Even with her haughtiness she was damn beautiful, he noted again. "You got anything you can wear riding a horse?" he asked her.

"Yes, in my things. I'll change in the general's office," she said.

"I'll get you an extra army mount," Fargo said and hurried to the camp stables. When he returned leading the brown standard army mount he saw her waiting, clothed in black riding britches and a dark blue, long-sleeved shirt that made her sun-dried wheat hair seem as though it were a yellow halo. She had a long cloth traveling bag which she tied to the mount's rump. She put one hand on the saddle horn to mount. "One minute," Fargo said. "I want to make sure you understand the ground rules."

"Ground rules?" she echoed with a tiny frown.

"Which are that you do whatever I tell you to do when I say it, no questions, no arguments. I say move fast you move fast. I say you move slow you move slow. I say lay on your belly, that's what you do. Climb a tree. You climb. Understood?"

The gray-blue eyes narrowed. "I don't take to being ordered about. Or haven't you ever used the word *please?*" she sniffed.

"Sure thing, honey, so here's what we do. Every time I give you an order you make believe I've said please." Fargo smiled almost affably. Her lips tightened as she swung onto the horse and he drank in the strong yet delicate odor, not unpleasant, yet very defined. "What do I smell?" he asked.

"A perfume brought to me from Paris. I know it's wasted out here in this wilderness but it makes me feel good to wear it," she said.

"Smells real nice," Fargo said as he pulled himself onto the Ovaro. "Let's go." He rode from the stockade with her and swore silently at Miles Stanford.

# 2

She rode well, Fargo noted, sitting the horse with ease. The army mount instantly knew it carried a different kind of rider, and as horses invariably do, tried to take charge. But Alison Carter was both sensitive and firm, and murmuring soothingly to the horse, she soon took command. She did it with understanding, patience, and warmth. It was quickly apparent that she reserved her haughty disdain for people. He had no objections. That was her privilege, except when it affected his neck. The scent of her kept drifting to him, quite a lovely scent, but his jaw grew tight as they rode. He set a path up into the low hills and he spotted the trails of unshod hoofprints.

He reined to a halt at one set of prints, dismounted, and pressed one hand to the marks. His lips drew back. "Fresh," he muttered as he swung back onto the Ovaro.

"How do you know?" Alison Carter asked.

"They're still moist," he answered.

"Shall we go another way?" she inquired.

"No point in it. They're all over these hills," he said. "We'll just be real careful and don't do anything stupid."

"I'd still feel safer with a platoon of troopers, despite General Stanford's confidence in you," Alison Carter sniffed.

"That makes us even. I'd feel safer without you," Fargo returned and led the way upward into hilly passages filled with the various shades of scarlet brilliance of butterfly weed, trumpet honeysuckle, and wood columbine. His eyes continued to sweep the terrain as they rode and the sun grew burning hot when he caught the silvery glint of water. He followed the path to find a small, high-ground pond, clear and shimmering blue, and he halted to let the horses drink. He swung from the saddle and watched Alison dismount with easy grace. "You've a washcloth in your things?" he asked.

"Of course," she said.

"Get it and wash all that damn perfume off yourself," he muttered.

She stared at him as though he'd said something childishly preposterous. "Absolutely not. Why would I want to do that?" she asked.

"So you don't bring the Cheyenne down on us," he said. "Or any other Indians that happen to be around."

"That's ridiculous. A little perfume? Nonsense," she said.

He clung to his patience though it took some effort as he held her with a long glance. "You went to school, a fancy school, I'd guess, the kind that keeps your nose up in the air."

"A rather quaint description but I suppose it fits in a way," Alison conceded.

"Well, out here you and your nose are in kindergarten. Take a deep breath. What do you smell?"

She inhaled and her breasts pressed tight against the dark blue shirt. "Trees, grass, fresh clean air," she said.

"Well, an Indian would smell the deer that passed this way not long ago. He'd smell the black-footed ferret that crossed into the trees and the black bear that came by. He'd smell the muskrat that's swimming at the other side of the pond. Shit, I smell them and he damn well would. He'd also smell the leather and polish of troopers if they'd come

*28*

this way and he'd smell the white folk scent of cotton and wool and he'd sure as hell smell that damn perfume of yours," Fargo said and drew a deep breath.

She eyed him, her lips pursed. "You're really impressed with all the things they say about the Indian, aren't you?" she commented.

"Yes, ma'am, yes, Jesus H. Christ indeed I am," Fargo said.

"You know what I think, Fargo? I think my perfume bothers you. It reminds you of dance-hall girls, though none of them has ever worn this, I'm sure. It makes you wish you were back with one of them right now. Well, you'll just have to exercise a little self-discipline," Alison answered.

"I take it that means you're not going to wash it off," Fargo said.

"That's right. I told you, wearing it helps me feel civilized out here," she said.

Fargo let out a deep sigh and the last of his patience left him with it. He started to turn away, suddenly spun, wrapped his arms around her, and lifted her from the ground. He swung her in a circle and she didn't get the chance to scream before she hit the pond with a loud splash. He followed in after her, wading almost to his waist as the bottom dropped quickly away, seized her and held her and held her under the water as he rubbed her long, smooth neck with one hand. He let her come up to the surface sputtering water and gasping for breath as he rubbed behind her ears. She swung at him, gasping. "Bastard," she managed before he pressed her under the surface of the water again.

He rubbed the sides and the back of her neck again with his hands, then down along her throat. Then he let her go and stepped back. She bobbed to the surface and clawed at him as she tried to curse with a mouthful of water. The wet shirt clung to her and revealed the contours of beautifully shaped, full breasts with very prominent nipples pushing against the fabric. "Now you won't be sending out signals," he said almost mildly.

"And now I'm soaking wet, you stupid oaf," Alison half screamed at him.

"In this sun you'll dry out in an hour," he said. He walked from the pond and pulled himself onto the Ovaro. Her eyes shot blue-gray fire at him from under the blond eyebrows as she followed and climbed onto her mount.

"I'll be telling the general about this," she said.

"You forgot the ground rules, honey. Don't forget them again," he said and sent the Ovaro forward in a walk. She came alongside him, her face no less beautiful for the simmering anger in it, the wet, flaxen hair glistening in the sun. He led the way around the pond, his eyes narrowed as they scanned every rise and hillock. His estimate had been accurate enough. Alison was pretty much dried out in a little over an hour, the shirt concealing again instead of revealing. She continued to ride in angry silence and that was fine with him. It let him concentrate on the lines of pony prints that crossed and crisscrossed the entire hill area. The damn territory was full of Indian bands.

The day slid into afternoon and a small forest of bur oak rose up before them and he moved carefully into it. They were deep into it when he halted and lifted one hand and Alison reined to a stop beside him. "Indians, about fifty yards up ahead," he half whispered.

"How do you know?" she questioned.

"Fish oil and bear grease. It works both ways," Fargo said and gestured to a dense cluster of trees within the forest. "Dismount and go into those trees, that thicket there. Stay there until I come back."

"What are you going to do?" Alison asked.

"See what we're up against," Fargo said. She nodded and

he waited till she had disappeared into the thicket, swallowed up by the foliage. He rode forward then another twenty-five yards before he dropped from the saddle. He left the Ovaro behind and went forward on foot. He heard them before he saw them and crept closer on cat's-paw steps until he dropped to one knee as they came into sight, a dozen near-naked bucks. He saw the carcass of a white-tail in one corner of the narrow clearing. A hunting party, preparing to bed down for the night. He grunted silently, swept the area again with a long glance, and moved backward to where he had left the Ovaro.

He rode back to the thicket in the waning day and she was standing, slightly apprehensive, as he came through the foliage. "Cheyenne, a hunting party," he said.

"That means they're not looking for us," she said.

"No, but they'd be real happy to hunt us," he said.

"What do we do? Go back?"

Fargo frowned for a long moment. "I don't like that. I saw too many other pony prints. We could run smack into another party. At least we know where these are."

"We go around them?" Alison asked.

"After they're asleep."

"Meanwhile?"

"We stay here," Fargo said. "Till night." He stretched out on his back in the thicket. "Get comfortable. We've a wait."

She sat down, her back against one of the trees. "I don't see why we just don't go around them now," she muttered.

"We could try, but what if one of our horses snorts? Or comes down on an old piece of branch and snaps it in two. That can sound like a .45 going off."

"It'd do that if they're asleep, too," Alison countered.

"That's why I'm going to give us some insurance," he said.

She frowned at him. "It seems to me you're being overly precautious," she sniffed.

"You're right. I sort of tend to do that when my scalp's on the line, seeing it's the only one I have," Fargo said.

She was silent for a moment. "You must understand, I'm accustomed to doing what I want when I want. I'm not used to this kind of thing," she said, a softness in her voice he'd not heard before.

"Is that an olive branch?" Fargo remarked.

"It's an explanation," she said, stiffness in her at once.

"Get some sleep. You'll need it tonight," he said and smiled as he closed his eyes and drew sleep around himself. He let himself sleep until the night was deep and he woke in the pitch blackness of the thicket. "Wake up, girl," he hissed and her voice came in moments, slurred with sleep at first, then clearing.

"I can't see a damn thing," she murmured. He rose, moved in the direction of her voice, hand outstretched. He found her hair and dropped his hand to her shoulder.

"Stay still, let your eyes adjust. It won't help much but it will some," he told her and in a few moments he felt his own vision respond, now able to distinguish darker shadows from the others. "This way," he said, holding her hand. The horses would follow, he knew, and when he emerged from the thicket with her he found that a weak moon filtered down enough wan light to let him see his way through the forest.

"Thank you," she said formally and drew her hand away. He moved forward on foot with Alison beside him and halted only when he was within a half-dozen yards of the sleeping forms. He pointed to a space between the oak near the edge of the cleared strip of land.

"That's north. When you hear a shot you ride through there and don't stop. If I haven't caught up to you by the time you reach the end of the forest you keep on riding. I'll find you," he told her. She nodded gravely and he led the Ovaro away, along the edge of the clear strip, and listened to the sounds of snoring and heavy breathing. He carefully circled to the other side of the strip and made his way back to where the Cheyenne had tethered their ponies. They used a typical loose Indian tether of a single length of hemp that they ran through the slack rope bridles. Fargo drew the double-edged throwing knife from the calf holster around his leg, cut the tether in two, and carefully pulled the lengths of rope until they came free. The Indian ponies were already backing up in sudden freedom when he drew the Colt and fired two shots in the air.

The ponies reacted at once, some bumping into each other as they whirled and then raced away. The shouts erupted at once as the braves snapped awake but Fargo was in the saddle and racing the Ovaro away. The Cheyenne had a moment of surprised confusion but, as he was certain they would, elected to run after their horses. Fargo sent the Ovaro through the oaks as fast as he dared, veered the horse to the right, and finally heard the sound of Alison's mount crashing through the forest ahead of him. He caught up to her as she reached the open land at the end of trees, came up alongside her, and waved her on. "Keep riding," he said, holding the Ovaro in a gallop for another fifteen minutes and then slowing to a canter and finally a trot.

"Aren't we going to stop?" she asked.

"Not till dawn," he said. "Those ponies won't run that far and when the Cheyenne catch them they'll come searching for whoever set them off. I want enough distance between us by then." She nodded and rode beside him and he maintained a steady pace through hill country that held a combination of wooded land and open stretches, high flat plateaus and sudden granite rock formations. The first streaks of pink were beginning to touch the horizon sky when he turned into a cluster of Rocky Mountain maple and dismounted. "We'll bed down here. It'll keep the morning sun from us and let us get some real sleep," he said. Alison took some things from her traveling bag and disappeared into the trees. Fargo laid out his bedroll and undressed down to his B.V.D.'s. He was stretched out atop the bedroll in the warm night when she returned in a pink, filmy nightgown, full-length, that might have been modest had it been of heavier material. But it clung to her as she moved and revealed a long line of thigh as well as the long curve of her breasts.

She caught his eyes as she drew a blanket from her things and put it on the ground. "Don't say it," she sniffed. "I'll get something more appropriate at whatever town's near the fort. I didn't expect I'd be roughing it."

"Fine with me," Fargo remarked.

"I'm sure it is," she tossed back tartly and wrapped herself in the blanket and lay down on her side. But he saw her eyes linger on the muscled symmetry of his naked torso before she turned on her back.

"Sleep well," he said.

"Hardly," she sniffed and he chuckled as he let slumber sweep through him. He stayed asleep until midmorning. He woke and was almost dressed when Alison stirred and sat up. The filmy pink nightgown was cut lower at the neck than he'd noticed in the dark and the fullness of one creamy breast pushed upward. Alison came fully awake and drew the blanket around herself as she went to her bag and into the trees. Fargo was using the water from his canteen to finish washing his face and torso when she returned. She went to the canteen on her mount and paused. "I'd like to do that if you'd turn your back," she said.

"Wouldn't think of it," he said. "But I am going to check things outside." He slipped on his shirt and strode from the maples to pause beyond in the bright sun, scanning the hills with a long, slow survey. A small herd of whitetail moved

*34*

in the distance, and a big black bear lumbered closer by. A flight of Bullock's orioles took wing to the right, no panic or fright in their movements. He nodded, satisfied, and returned to where Alison waited in the maples, her peaches-and-cream complexion glowing and scrubbed. "Let's ride," he said and she followed him out as he turned the Ovaro northeast. He held a brisk pace through the heat of the day. She refused to complain but she was plainly grateful for a halt at a clear hill stream.

The day began to dip to an end when he saw the tall peaks of the Medicine Bow Mountains rise in the distance and he turned north along a worn trail. Following the directions General Stanford had given him, he made his way to lower ground and was surprised to see the buildings of a town rise up a few hundred yards ahead. A crude wooden signpost marked the entrance to the town with the words OLD GABE carved into the wood.

"Strange name for a town," Alison sniffed.

"Not if you know what it means. Old Gabe was the nickname for mountain man Jim Bridger," Fargo explained as they moved into the town, a single, wide street with wood and clapboard buildings on both sides, a typical town but established enough to have a general store and a rooming house along with the staple dance hall. Alison slowed before the rooming house.

"I'd like to spend the night in a bed," she said.

Fargo mused for a moment, aware they had no chance of reaching the army camp until the next afternoon. He also welcomed the chance to ask questions of the townsfolk. "Why not?" he said and Alison halted and slid from the mount.

"I presume they'll have a room. Shall I get you one?" she asked.

"I'll pick one up later if I'm so inclined," he said.

"Where are you going now?" she asked.

"To the dance hall," Fargo said.

"I might have known," she sniffed disdainfully.

"See you come morning," he said. "Unsaddle your mount before you turn in." She hurried into the small rooming house and Fargo rode on as the night fell and reined up outside the saloon and dance hall. Inside, he found it a typical saloon, a handful of girls in too-bright dresses with searching eyes, a pockmarked bar presided over by a stocky man with short, graying hair. Fargo ordered a bourbon and a buffalo sandwich. He sat at the bar and let the bartender strike up the conversation.

"Just passing through," he said in answer to the usual question. "Didn't expect to find a town this size around here," he commented.

"It's the only one. We serve all the settler families in the low hills north. They come all the way down for houseware and clothing items," the bartender said. "Of course, you go west and east there are a half-dozen towns, but they're mostly made up of saloons and trapper supplies."

"The army camp boys visit you?" Fargo asked.

"Not a lot. They mostly go for the saloon towns along the west line," the man said. "You haven't asked about the name so I expect you know what it means. Jim Bridger used to pass this way a lot."

"Been hearing about Indian trouble. You know anything about it?" Fargo asked casually.

"Yes, up north of the Little Snake, past the army compound," the bartender said.

"You know anything about General Carter?" Fargo asked.

"He's never come to town but I hear he runs a lot of patrols, his way of keeping a tight rein on the Cheyenne," the man said.

Fargo caught the inflection in the man's voice. "You don't think much of the idea?" he questioned.

"There's keeping a tight rein and there's riling them up," the bartender said grimly. "It can be a damn thin line."

"I'm sure of that. Thanks for the conversation," Fargo said as he paid his tab and walked from the saloon. Outside, he walked the Ovaro to the boardinghouse, remembering what Miles had said about General Wendell Carter. Maybe that's all it was, an echo of the bartender's words, a misfit martinet trying to assert his authority. Maybe nothing more than that, Fargo mused and hoped real hard he was right. He halted in front of the boardinghouse, the frown suddenly deep into his brow, and then he was stalking past the army mount and into the house. An elderly man with a green eyeshade and a bald head looked up from the front desk. "The young woman who took a room a few hours ago," Fargo bit out, "what room was it?"

"I don't give out that kind of information, mister," the man said.

"I appreciate that. I don't aim to hurt her any. She just forgot something I have to remind her about," Fargo said.

The old man thought for a moment, took in the hard line of Fargo's jaw. "Room 4, end of hall," he muttered.

"Much obliged," Fargo said as he strode down the hallway to the last room. Closing his hand around the doorknob, he turned slowly and the door opened. He stepped into the almost dark room, a sliver of moonlight coming in through a lone window. He walked toward the bed, making no effort to be silent, and Alison Carter woke. She sat up and he saw she wore the pink nightgown as he yanked her from the bed.

"What are you doing, damn you?" she flung at him as she stood beside the bed.

"Put a robe on," he snapped and she reached out to the end of the bed and drew on a light silk robe. "Come on," he growled, pulling her along by one wrist, out of the room and down the hall and outside into the night. He halted before the army mount. "You didn't take the saddle off that horse. Do it, now," he ordered.

"I forgot," she said.

"Bullshit. You didn't forget," he snapped. "You didn't pay attention to what I said. Get it off now, dammit."

"You're mad, do you know that?" Alison said. She began to unsaddle the horse until finally she had the saddle on the ground and her breath came in deep gasps.

"One more lesson, honey," Fargo said. "Out here your horse isn't something you just ride on and enjoy. Out here your horse is part of you. It can save your life, get you to where you have to go, be your friend and companion, sometimes be a lot more trustworthy and faithful than people. Your horse needs care, attention, time to rest without a weight on its back. Out here you take care of your horse before you take care of yourself." He paused and she continued to glare at him. "Now take your saddle inside with you. Saddles are valuable out here."

She grunted as she lifted the saddle and half dragged, half carried it into the boardinghouse, not looking back at him. He waited till he heard the door to her room slam shut and then took a room for himself across from hers. He undressed at once, the Ovaro's saddle beside him, and fell asleep in the luxury of a bed. The daylight woke him and he washed and dressed and went outside to find Alison putting the saddle on her mount. She had changed into a dark green shirt and with her flaxen hair the color combination made her look like a wood sorrel. She finished and turned to him as he tightened the cinch under the Ovaro's belly.

"I'm sorry about last night, about the saddle," she said and he peered at her for a moment.

"Good," he said.

"Must you always teach your lessons so harshly?"

"Folks remember them better that way," he said and

swung onto the pinto. She rode beside him as he struck out northward, the land rising, good land with plenty of rich soil and black oak, cottonwoods and red cedar. Below and in the distance, he glimpsed the curving upper reaches of the Little Snake River. They had stopped to let the horses drink twice and the day had slid into midafternoon when the buildings came into view some few hundred yards ahead and he followed as Alison put her mount into a trot.

"What did General Stanford mean when he said my father wouldn't be wanting my visit now?" she asked as they neared the buildings.

"I don't know," Fargo said blandly.

"You're lying," she tossed at him.

"What did you mean when you said you couldn't wait for him to want a visit from you?" Fargo questioned.

"That didn't mean anything," Alison said.

"Now who's lying?" Fargo returned. She turned angry eyes on him and then he saw them soften and he laughed, a low, rich sound. "Perhaps we ought to start being honest with each other," she said.

"Not a bad idea," he agreed and brought his attention back to the scene in front of him. The army camp was a compound, at best, a high-walled stockade with corner guard platforms. He saw a half-dozen small buildings inside the square compound, one plainly a barracks, two more supply sheds, one a stable and the others officers' quarters with the company flag flying atop one. But nearly half the squad was bivouacked in tents outside the compound, along with a roped-off area for their horses. A strange place, Fargo commented silently, more of a glorified field post than a proper army stockade. He spied a few one-horse huckster wagons, some with produce still inside their high sides, and seven-inch floor boards. The post received supplies from local farmers, he took note as he and Alison drew up before the building flying the post flag.

A corporal with a carbine stood guard outside and watched them dismount. "I'll go in alone first," Fargo muttered to Alison, who hesitated a moment and then agreed with a nod. He stepped up to the trooper. "General Carter, soldier," he said. "General Miles Stanford sent me." The trooper nodded, disappeared into the house for a moment, and returned.

"General Carter's waiting," he said and Fargo gave Alison a quick glance as he strode into the small building. He found himself in a fair-sized room, a desk and a file cabinet against one wall, three straight-backed chairs near the desk, and the officer standing behind the desk staring at him with cold, blue-gray eyes. Fargo was instantly struck by the man's features, stronger and more masculine that Alison's but otherwise with the same evenness, the same fair coloring, dark blond hair flecked with gray. The same cool disdain in his manner, too, Fargo noted, but while Alison's airs were learned, he had decided, General Wendell Carter's disdain came from inside him, the iciness of it deep in his eyes.

"Fargo, Skye Fargo," the Trailsman said and drew the letter from General Stanford from his pocket and put it on the desk, where Wendell Carter picked it up, opened it, and read it quickly. Fargo watched the man's jaw muscles grow tight as he finished.

"The esteemed Major General Stanford has his goddamn nerve sending a civilian up here to check on me," Wendell Carter rasped.

"I wouldn't look at it that way, sir," Fargo offered soothingly.

"How the hell am I supposed to look at it?" General Carter snapped.

"As General Stanford just doing his job, getting his own firsthand report, and offering you my help," Fargo said.

"I don't need your help, Fargo. The best thing you can do is turn around and ride out of here," the general barked.

" 'Fraid I can't be doing that," Fargo said. "I can't report to General Stanford until I've satisfied myself."

"There's nothing for you to see, dammit," Carter roared. "And I give the orders around here."

It was time to stop trying to soothe a man who wasn't about to be soothed, Fargo decided. "You don't give orders to me, General. I'm not one of your soldier boys," he said, his voice hardening. Wendell Carter's eyes were narrowed slits as they bored into the big man in front of him.

"Anything else, Fargo?" he asked.

"Just so happens there is," Fargo said. "Be right back." He spun on one heel, strode outside and returned leading Alison, to see General Wendell Carter's jaw drop in astonishment.

"Hello, Father," Alison said calmly.

Fargo watched the general's lips twitch, his face grow an angry red, and little sounds stammer from his mouth. General Carter's voice finally gathered itself and the astonishment turned into a frown of disbelief. "What are you doing here, Alison?" he barked.

"I came to see you and you know why," Alison said and Fargo heard the ice in her voice.

"Did you pay this man to bring you here?" the general thrust at her, waving a hand at Fargo.

"No. I wanted an escort from General Stanford. He claimed he couldn't provide me with one and he said I could go along with Fargo," Alison answered and her father spun on the big man standing by.

"You can take her right back, you hear me?" he shouted.

"I'm not going right back, remember?" Fargo said calmly. "She knew that."

"And I'm not going back till I get what I came for," Alison said to her father.

*41*

General Carter's eyes stayed on Fargo. "Get out. I've personal things to discuss with Alison but I'll be talking to you tomorrow," the man said.

"I expect so," Fargo said and walked from the room, aware that he left Alison and her father staring at each other with anger. He walked outside and led the Ovaro from the stockade as dusk settled in to quickly turn to night. He walked beyond the line of troopers in their tents to a small rise, plentiful with shadbush. He unsaddled the horse and sat down to a small fire and heated some lengths of beef jerky from his saddlebag.

Miles Stanford had been wrong about one thing so far. General Carter hadn't been at all grateful for having his daughter arrive safely. There'd be no cooperation from him because of that. Sitting back against the smooth, gray-brown bark of a shadbush, Fargo put aside speculating about the man's reaction; only time would give it dimension. He relaxed against the tree, his eyes half closed. The small cookfires by the trooper's tents had all but died away when he glimpsed the dark form moving past the rear of the tents and up the incline toward him, a lone horse and rider, and he sat up straighter. The shape grew and became Alison Carter and she halted before him and slid to the ground, her flaxen hair a pale yellow in the moonlight.

"I saw the fire up here and guessed it might be you," she said.

"Have a nice talk with Daddy?" Fargo inquired.

"Hardly," she said. "I knew he wasn't going to be happy to see me but I didn't think he'd be this mad. I've only seen him this angry once before, when Mother found out something he didn't want her to know."

"Did you find out something he didn't want you to know?" Fargo queried.

"No. The only thing I found out is that he's going to be more uncooperative than I expected he'd be," Alison said.

"About what?"

"Family business. I don't think I should talk about it, not yet, anyway. Part of his attitude is your fault, I think," Alison said and Fargo let his brows lift. "I got the feeling he's real angry about your being here, for whatever reasons."

"For whatever reasons," Fargo echoed.

"I've been given my own quarters in one of the cabins inside the stockade," Alison told him.

""I wouldn't expect less," Fargo said.

"I don't intend to be a prisoner," she said.

"You think that's what he has in mind?"

"I wouldn't put anything past him," Alison said coldly and took a step closer, her voice softening. "Thanks for getting me here. I know I haven't been very gracious but I am grateful." He regarded her with a long stare. "What are you thinking?" she asked.

"I'm wondering if you really are grateful or are you afraid you're going to need a friend," Fargo said.

Her eyes narrowed for a moment and she tensed, but he saw her shoulders relax. "I won't lie to you. Maybe some of both," she said.

"I'll accept that," he said, not unkindly.

"What will you be doing now?" Alison asked.

"Ride, poke around, ask questions, watch my ass," Fargo said. "You want me to check in on you when I've a chance?"

"Yes, I'd like that," she said solemnly. He nodded and she turned and started down the hillside, the darkness giving her an ethereal quality. When she was swallowed up by the night he undressed and stretched out on his bedroll. He went to sleep convinced that Wendell Carter was going to be a problem. The only question was how much of one.

# 3

Fargo faced General Wendell Carter soon after the morning dawned. He had leisurely washed and dressed, rode the pinto down the hill, and started past the stockade gate when the two troopers halted him. "The general wants to see you, mister," one of the soldiers said.

Fargo had regarded the trooper. "That a request or an order, soldier?" he'd asked.

The soldier half shrugged and looked uncomfortable. "I don't know but we take most everything the general says as an order," he answered.

"I'll take it as a request," Fargo said and followed the trooper into the office, where General Carter closed the door after the soldier left.

"I'll come right to the point, Fargo," the general said, his voice tight. "I want Alison out of here. You managed to bring her here so I'm assuming you can take her back. I'll pay you five hundred dollars to do that, immediately, today."

Fargo let a low whistle escape his lips. "That's a lot of money," he commented.

"It is, but money's important to men such as you," the general said, not hiding the disdain in his voice.

"You're right there," Fargo agreed affably.

"Good. We've a deal, as I expected," General Carter said.

"Expect again," Fargo said and Carter's brow furrowed. "As I see it, it's take Alison away and get me out of your hair at the same time, killing two birds with one stone."

"You could put it that way," Carter muttered.

"Only I've a job to do for General Stanford. Sorry, but it's no deal," Fargo said.

The general's face grew a deep red. "You'll be sorry you didn't take my offer, Fargo," he rasped.

"Why don't you just tell me what's going on around here, save us both a lot of time and trouble, and maybe I can take Alison back," Fargo said.

"There's nothing going on here I can't handle," Carter thundered. "You interfere with army business in any way I'll have you clapped in the guardhouse and be damned with Miles Stanford."

"I'll remember that," Fargo said nonchalantly and felt the man's glare boring into his back as he walked from the office. Alison was outside as he climbed onto the Ovaro and he saw the questions in her eyes. "You owe me five hundred dollars," he said cheerfully.

"What are you talking about?" Alison frowned.

"Ask Daddy," he said, laughed, and waved as he sent the Ovaro from the stockade at a trot. He turned the horse north by west, rode along a worn trail that bordered hill country, and slowed as he came upon a funeral procession, less than a handful of mourners following an old furniture wagon with wide, open slat sides that carried not furniture but six pine box coffins. Four gravediggers carrying shovels followed along behind and Fargo drew up alongside the men. "Whose funeral?" he asked.

"Settler folk from the hill country. Tenth one we've had this month," one of the men answered. "And I hear they had three more out of Boulder Rock." Fargo glanced at the six pine boxes again. "Sarah Taylor, Mary and Irma

Cozzins, and the three Fowler women, two grown daughters and their ma," the man said.

"None of their men?" Fargo frowned.

"Their men were all in Old Gabe and Boulder Rock picking up supplies when the Cheyenne hit, damn them," another of the diggers put in. "Bill Taylor and Sam Cozzins have already packed to leave. I'd guess Ed Fowler will be doing the same."

"Much obliged," Fargo said and rode on, a new grimness gathering inside him. The Cheyenne were raiding, in their usual ruthless fashion. Carter had to know about it. Was that what he didn't want General Stanford to know about? Did he want to handle it all on his own? It didn't make a whole lot of sense, Fargo pondered. Stanford would understand a rash of Cheyenne raids. He knew the Indians couldn't be completely shut down. Or was there something more Carter wanted to keep to himself? The frown stayed with him as Fargo turned the pinto into the high country. He'd ridden another quarter-mile or so when he came to a house, well made with the eight-by-eights joined with tenons and mortises. Beyond it lay a field plowed and cut and planted with crops growing well. He saw lettuce and squash, tuber vines and rows of string beans. He reined to a halt but no one came out of the open door of the house.

He called out but silence was the only reply and he slid from the saddle and walked around to the rear of the house. There was no wagon, no extra plow horse, only the broken wheel of a surrey. The place seemed deserted and, one hand on the butt of the big Colt at his hip, he went around to the front of the house and stepped inside. A large single room greeted him, part kitchen and part living room. But it had been emptied. The shelves along the walls were empty save for a few trenchers and an iron stew pot. Only the frame of a trundle bed remained, the mattress and sheets removed, and then he saw the piece of paper on the block table, a knife sticking through it to hold it in place. He stepped up to it and left it with the knife in it as he began to read.

> To whosoever comes by:
> This here house and land is yours for the taking. You can keep this here letter as your deed. I have decided to go back East since my Nora was killed by the Cheyenne. It's not just the heartache but I've two four-year-old boys to raise and a man can't work the land, hunt for food and keep a place in fit condition and raise two little children.
> Maybe I'll come back another time to another place when the boys have growed some but now I'm leaving. There's nothin' else to do.
>
> Amos Hardy

Fargo walked from the house and rode on, a sadness wrapping itself around him. A passing tragedy, one of so many in this untamed land, and yet it seemed somehow more, a special quality to it. Perhaps because of the funeral procession of the six women he had just passed, he reflected, and sent the pinto into a canter. He rode north, higher into the hill country, and drew on memory to find his way. It had been a few years since he'd come this way and he could only hope that Willie still lived in his own little ravine in the hills. He and Willie had worked together often enough in years past, sometimes for Miles Stanford. Willie had been one of the general's best scouts. Half Cheyenne and half Arikara, the troopers had immediately named him Willie Moccasin and the name stuck and no one any longer remembered his tribal name. Fargo saw the twisted trunk of the Rocky Mountain maple, turned the Ovaro to follow the narrow pathway the circled to the left of the trunk and in minutes the long, narrow ravine came into sight.

Fargo nosed the pinto down the mouth of the ravine, which was partially obscured by thick serviceberry, and the narrow house appeared minutes later and he was glad to see the sliver of smoke rising from the chimney. As he rode up to the door the man came outside, a small and wiry figure in faded jeans and the dark brown leather vest Fargo remembered was always part of his attire. The man stared at Fargo, who noted that his dark-complexioned, sun-worn face had gathered a few more lines but his step was still spry. "Fargo . . . Skye Fargo. I'll be damned," Willie Moccasin breathed.

"Hello, old friend," Fargo smiled as he dismounted, and Willie stepped forward to clasp his hand. "You look well."

"Feel good," Willie said. Fargo's eyes moved past Willie Moccasin to the pottery shed behind the house and some pottery wheels outside it. When General Stanford moved to a new command Willie decided he'd had his fill of scouting. He got the house here in the ravine and made a living selling craft work, pottery, urns, and woven rugs, much of which he made himself. He'd supplemented his income with an occasional scouting job when he needed it.

"Still turning out the pieces, I see," Fargo said, and Willie nodded as Fargo gazed past the shed to the shallow, tree-lined ravine. Everything was as he remembered it.

"Come in, old friend. This calls for a drink," Willie said and Fargo followed him into the long house comfortably furnished with blankets, a single sofa, and numerous padded leather pillows for sitting on the floor. Fargo folded himself onto one as Willie brought out a tan clay jug and held it up.

"Same good whiskey?" Fargo asked and the Indian nodded as he poured two clay cups and held his up in a toast. "To old times, old friends, and old memories," Fargo said.

"Good enough, Fargo," Willie said as they drank and the richly mellow whiskey was its own memory as Fargo savored it, a brandy and sherry mixture some monks had taught Willie how to make. "What brings you visiting, Fargo?" Willie asked.

"General Stanford pointed me in this direction," Fargo said and quickly told him of the general's concerns. "You know this man Carter?" he asked Willie.

"I see him sometimes," Willie said and Fargo smiled. He had long ago learned to read the subtleties in Willie's voice others only found flat.

"And you don't like him," Fargo smiled.

"I see hard outside, soft inside," Willie said.

"You know the Cheyenne have been raiding, hitting hard," Fargo said and Willie nodded. "What else do you know?" Fargo asked.

"Cheyenne chief is strong man called Night Claw," Willie said. "Good man to stay away from."

"You still have your contacts in the tribes," Fargo said and Willie's half shrug was an admission. "Find out what you can for me," Fargo said. "General Carter is not happy that I came here. I'd like to know why. Maybe you can find out something, old friend."

"I live here and nobody bothers me because I do not bother anybody," Willie said. "I do not want this Cheyenne chief Night Claw coming after me."

"I understand that, Willie," Fargo said as he finished his drink. "I don't want that, either. But you know how to ask and how to listen." The wiry little man said nothing and continued to look unhappy. "General Stanford gave me money to pay. It will not be just for old times' sake," Fargo added.

Willie Moccasin refilled the clay cups. "No promises, old friend," he said.

"No promises. Just search the wind," Fargo said and the Indian almost smiled.

"Let us talk of old times, now," Willie said and Fargo joined him in a deep draught of the warm, rich liquid. They did talk of old times and the night came and finally Fargo rose. "You can stay here," Willie said.

"Next time, perhaps," Fargo said. "I want to be in the low hills when dawn comes." He clasped hands with Willie again and rode slowly from the half-hidden ravine under an almost full moon. Riding downward into the low hill country, he camped under a cottonwood and slept till the morning sun woke him. He found a stream in which to wash and he was riding the Ovaro at a walk as the sun began to climb through the sky, his eyes scanning the terrain. He halted under a shade tree when the noon hour arrived, rested the horse, and later moved on again to turn when he spied a thin column of dust to the east. He rode toward it, staying higher in the fairly thick tree cover until he was able to see down onto a high plain where a squad of soldiers were riding escort for a wagon, a hay wagon but without hay inside its long, upswept body. Instead, eight young woman were seated inside the wagon, which was driven by a man wearing a wide-brimmed Stetson and overalls. Fargo's eyes swept the squad of troopers again and he counted ten, one carrying the company pennant, which read Squad 4.

He swung the Ovaro around and paralleled the troopers with the wagon below as he stayed inside the line of black oak. He had stayed with the wagon perhaps another quarter mile when he caught the movement of the trees to his left and reined to a halt. Sidling deeper into the trees, he peered forward and saw the distant branches move again in a straight line. He edged the horse forward, his eyes narrowed, and suddenly he caught the silent forms moving behind the trees, loin-clothed braves moving silently in single file down toward the open plains below. Fargo sent the Ovaro sideways, where he could see down to the flatland. The troopers were riding alongside the wagon, a corporal out in front.

The Indians had disappeared from his sight but he knew they were below, almost where the trees ended at the edge of the plain, and he drew the Colt from its holster. There was no time for him to ride down and warn the escorting troopers. There was only one way to alert them and he raised the gun into the air and fired off three shots. He saw the squad rein to a halt, all eyes peering up into the trees, and then he saw the racing, near-naked horsemen charge out onto the plains. He made a fast count and came up with twelve. Then he started to send the Ovaro downhill, when he suddenly yanked the horse to a halt. The troopers hadn't sent the long wagon racing forward. It was still at a dead stop. They weren't dismounting, waving the women out to turn the wagon over and take a stand behind it. It was long enough and heavy enough to afford a good fighting barrier. Instead they were milling about, firing off shots at the charging Indians, who had spread out as they charged. Cheyenne, Fargo grimaced as he caught the decoration on the armband one wore.

The attackers were closing in, firing both rifles and arrows and Fargo heard the curse fall from his lips as the troopers fell back, turned at orders from the corporal, and began to race away. "Jesus, no," Fargo heard himself shouting. "You could make those boxelders over there." But the ten troopers were fleeing, racing their mounts away, and Fargo saw the Cheyenne halt when they reached the wagon. They fired a few more rounds at the fleeing troopers but made no effort to pursue them. Instead, they pulled the young women from the hay wagon, flung them to the ground, bashed the heads in on two, and pulled the others away from the wagon. They bound their wrists with rawhide, set fire to the wagon, and climbed onto their ponies to ride away, dragging the six women after them.

The troopers had disappeared, though Fargo had peered after them, hoping they might return charging. But they didn't and he heard himself still cursing. It had been more than panic, more than ineptness. It had been cowardice and he'd have a few things to tell Carter. But that could wait.

Right now he had to see if he could help six young women and his lips pulled back at the thought. The chances were not good, he realized all too well, but he stayed in the oak as he followed the Cheyenne. The dozen braves stayed on the plain for another hour, not turning into the hill country until the sun was beginning to move down toward the horizon line. Fargo pulled a little closer to the Cheyenne as they moved along the hill trails, dragging their captives behind them. He saw two of the women being pulled along the ground, over ridges, screaming with pain at each rock but no longer able to walk.

Fargo cursed with the feeling of utter helplessness but knew he had to wait. Dusk settled over the hill country, became night, and finally Fargo smelled the odors of cooking fires and meat roasting. He still followed behind the Cheyenne band and stayed on their heels until the camp opened up and the Indians rode in with their captives. Fargo swung to the ground and crept forward on foot, positioning himself behind the thick trunk of an oak, where he could take in the entire camp. No line camp, he saw at once, but a base camp replete with numerous teepees, skin-drying racks, squaws and naked children and a stream along one side. He dropped to one knee as the six women were untied and immediately set on by a cluster of old squaws, who spat and struck at them as they pulled their clothes off.

The women were naked in minutes, two still in torn bloomers, all on the ground, some curled up as the squaws beat them with thin birch sticks. At a sound, the squaws fell back and a half-circle of braves and younger women wearing only hide skirts, formed around the six captives as Fargo saw the tall figure approach. The man wore a necklace of wild turkey claws hanging around his neck, his bare torso bronzed and muscular, his loins encased in buckskin leggings. He had the high forehead of the Cheyenne, his black hair worn almost shoulder length, and befitting the tallest of the plains tribes, he stood six feet in height. Fargo's eyes held the Indian's face and took in the imperiousness mixed with cruelty, the wide mouth turning down at the corners. Even without the deference of the others, he had no need to wonder who the Indian was and the words formed silently on his lips: Night Claw.

While two of the braves stepped forward, the Cheyenne chief pointed to one of the six women, a dark-haired girl with a full figure and heavy breasts. Two two braves seized her by the arms and held her and Night Claw steppled forward, lifted her legs, and burst forth from his leggings and plunged into her as she screamed. He took her with brutal force and all she could do was scream and twist her torso as she was held and then she was turned over and he took her again from behind. Two of the other women tried to rush at the chief but were immediately kicked away by other young bucks. Fargo felt his hand clutch tight around the Colt and forced his fingers to draw back. There was nothing he could do to help the woman, not yet. Any attempt would end in his own capture.

Finally the Cheyenne chief stepped back and let the young woman fall to the ground, where she lay moaning. He held out his hand and one of the young bucks placed a skinning knife in it. As Fargo watched in horror, Night Claw reached down and slashed the woman's throat with one sweeping blow. Fargo knew the Colt was in his hand and his arm was trembling as he forced himself not to fire and he watched in surprise as the Cheyenne chief lifted his arms high in the air and the others dropped to their knees. He intoned words in a deep, rumbling voice and Fargo, his Algonkian rudimentary at best, could only catch a few phrases, but the horror had suddenly become some sort of worship ceremony. The moment ended as abruptly as it had begun and Night Claw strode majestically to the large teepee at one end of the camp. The other braves fell on the remaining five women, beating them as they raped them and Fargo turned away and gritted his teeth as he couldn't shut out the screams.

But finally the screams ended and Fargo lifted himself from one knee to peer into the camp again. Three of the women lay lifeless on the ground, their naked bodies torn with cuts and swollen with massive bruises. As he watched, they were dragged to one side of the camp and tossed in a gruesome tangle of naked limbs. The remaining two women, brutally beaten but still alive, were pulled to the other edge of the camp and bound to stakes by rawhide thongs. It was apparent they were to be saved for more brutal pleasure in the morning as the Indian camp began to settle down for the night. Most of the squaws and children retired to teepees, as did a number of the braves. But not all. The others lay down in the open and were quickly asleep. But Fargo waited another hour before starting the long, stealthy trek around the edged of the Cheyenne camp.

When he reached the stakes where the two remaining women were tied he felt his lips draw back as he saw how badly they had been beaten and mutilated. But they were still alive and he paused, scanning the camp. He saw only sleeping figures and crept forward on his stomach. Using the double-edged throwing knife in the calf holster around his leg, he cut the rawhide thongs and both the women managed to open their eyes to stare at him. he gently put his hand across the first girl's mouth, then the second, and comprehension slowly came into their battered faces. Helping them to crawl, pulling first one then the other, he reached the brush surrounding the camp and let them gasp in breath. "I can't . . . I can't," one of the girls breathed through puffed lips.

"Yes, you can," Fargo whispered. "What's your name?"

"Christy," she managed to say.

"Hold on, Christy. We'll make it," he told her and glanced at the other young woman. She lay with her eyes half open and he ran his hand across her forehead. "You will, too," he told her. "I'll see that you make it. Come on, crawl, slowly, just don't give up." He positioned himself between the two young women and held each by one arm as he helped them move forward, pausing every few minutes. Christy managed to move forward by the sheer determination to survive but the other young woman moved only with his aid. He halted to let them rest for longer periods every five minutes, although they hadn't reached the end of the Cheyenne camp.

Christy lay breathing in deep draughts of air while the other girl's chest hardly moved. "What's her name?" he asked Christy.

"Inez," Christy murmured.

Fargo leaned his face down to the other girl. "We'll make it, Inez. Don't give up now, you hear me?" he said. Her eyes flickered but there was no answer and he turned back to Christy. "Ready to go on?" he asked and his stomach curled at the terrible pain he saw cross her face.

"Not yet," she said and her eyes began to close. He pressed her shoulder. He had to keep her awake.

"Talk to me, Christy," he said. "Where were you going?"

"Army," she breathed, her lids still drooping, and he pressed her shoulder again.

"Where were you from?" he asked.

"Denville," she said.

"You lived in Denville?"

"Saloon . . . bar girls."

"You were all dancehall girls?" Fargo frowned and she nodded. He didn't ask more. She was awake enough and he turned and closed his hand around Inez's arm and gently pulled. She didn't respond and he bent to her and slowly raised his head. "Goddamn," he whispered. "Goddamn."

He turned and began to crawl forward again with Christy. They reached the one end of the Cheyenne camp and he rested again before starting to circle. If they could reach the Ovaro he'd put her across the saddle and conserve what little strength she had left. But his eyes moved through the light and suddenly the Ovaro seemed a long way away. Another glance at Christy made him decide to take the risk. "You stay here," he said and a terrible relief managed to show through her battered face. He left her lying on her side and began to move along the far edge of the camp. Bringing the horse back, no matter how carefully he did it, would be a precarious piece of business. Yet it was the only way the young woman could make it, he realized. There was no way the Ovaro's big bulk could move through the thick trees in silence. He could only hope the Cheyenne remained in a deep sleep.

He was halfway around the far end of the camp when he heard the shout split the night, then another, and he cursed. Someone had woken and found the two girls gone. He turned and, running in a crouch, made his way back to where Christy lay as he heard the sound of voices. The camp was now fully awake. They'd see the trail where he'd crawled with the two young women and be at him in minutes. He cursed again as he dropped to one knee beside Christy and began to lift her. "No, God, no," she gasped out. "I hurt too much, inside. I can't make it."

"You can. You have to," Fargo hissed and began to lift her again and she cried out in pain.

"No, please," she said. "I can't. You can't with me. It's too late. It's over. Run. Get out of here."

He heard the Cheyenne moving through the trees and knew she was right and lowered her against a tree trunk. He felt her move, lift one arm half around him, and he held her for another second and she fell back and in horror he saw his Colt in her hand. She found the strength to pull the trigger and her temple exploded in a shower of blood and bone and she fell sideways. Cursing, silent, bitter curses, he pulled the gun from her hand and ran, racing through the brush now, back toward where he had left the Ovaro.

The Cheyenne were on foot and they'd halt when they found the first girl, then the second. It would be enough time for him to get a good start. He reached the horse, leaped into the saddle and sent the pinto through the trees in as fast a gallop as he dared. He turned right, then left, then right again, to leave a zigzag trail they'd have to slow down to follow. Chances were they wouldn't try to follow until dawn and he'd be far away by then. He settled down, slowed to a fast canter, and let the Ovaro find its way in the moonlight until he reached open land. He cut across the plain, then, and finally downward again until he halted beneath a wide bur oak, unsaddled the horse, and stretched out atop his bedroll. There was time for a few hours of sleep before morning, when the first order of business would be to tell a stiff-backed general that one of his squads was made of cowards.

He grimaced as he thought about the young women and wondered what an army patrol was doing escorting a wagonload of saloon girls. The question hung in his mind as he went to sleep knowing that the frustrating horror of this night would long linger inside him.

# 4

The sun woke him and he tried to wash away the sourness inside him at a clear stream, only to find it wouldn't wash away and finally he rode from the hills with memories of the night clinging to him. When he finally arrived at the stockade he saw Alison striding from the general's office, her face tight. She paused as she saw him halt and swing to the ground.

"Trouble with Daddy?" he remarked.

"Don't call him that," she spit back. "He's a stubborn, arrogant man who refuses to listen to anyone else."

"Kind of like his daughter?" Fargo said. Her mouth fell open as she glared at him but she pulled it closed without answering and strode away, her firm, flat rear barely moving inside the black riding britches. Fargo continued on into the general's office where Wendell Carter looked up from behind his desk, his uniform crisply pressed, his face wearing faint disdain.

"Unless you've something important, I'm busy," Wendell Carter said.

"It's important," Fargo said grimly. "You've got a troop of yellow-livered cowards riding for you."

The general's eyes narrowed at him. "You'd better have a damn good reason for that kind of talk, Fargo," he said tightly.

"I damn well do," Fargo returned. "I saw your Squad 4

abandon a wagon of eight women when a Cheyenne band attacked. They could have made a stand or they could have reached a cluster of box elder. They didn't do either. They just ran. They left those poor women for the Cheyenne. Goddamn cowards, all of them."

"They may have had a good reason. I don't take to my men being called cowards," Carter said.

"Reason, shit. There weren't that many Cheyenne. They just took off and ran, I'm telling you, the corporal leading them," Fargo said.

"That'd be Corporal Bender," the general said. "I'll question him on this. I'll look into it."

"Look into it? Hell, I'm telling you what I saw. I want those men brought up on charges."

Carter's face hardened. "I'll decide what disciplinary actions are needed, if any. I don't need you to tell me how to run my command, Fargo."

Fargo felt the fury coursing through him at the man's haughty attitude. "You damn well better decide right," he growled.

"Are you daring to threaten me?" Carter shot back.

"That's not a threat. That's just advice," Fargo said with steely calm.

"Anything else, mister?" the general said, his face an icy mask.

"Yes. What was an army troop doing escorting eight saloon girls?" Fargo questioned.

"I don't know but I can make a guess," Carter said.

"Such as?"

"Squad 4 came upon them, and knowing the Cheyenne have been raiding, offered them protection."

"Some goddamn protection," Fargo bit out as he strode from the office.

Outside, he swung onto the Ovaro and rode from the stockade. The general's answer had had the sweet sound of reasonableness, he realized, but something was wrong. Carter had been defensive, but he'd expected that. Miles Stanford had described Carter as a misfit. Men like that were always defensive and usually martinets, an effort to cover up their own insecurity. But that still wasn't enough. Fargo frowned and suddenly came onto what speared at him. Carter had shown bluster, hostility, and defensiveness. But no surprise. Did he know Squad 4 was made up of cowards? Or did he know they merely reflected his inability to command, to instill the right things in his men? Was that what he feared, being reported back to Miles Stanford? Was his entire command riddled with morale problems?

The questions were all possible and yet they failed to satisfy, Fargo muttered silently as he rode into the hills. There was more, something hidden away. He felt it inside himself and he put aside further speculation until he had something more concrete. The land lay under a warm sun and seemed tranquil, but he knew the deception in its lush beauty. He'd work his way to Willie Moccasin later. He wanted to ride the high land in the daylight again and explore further and he made a slow circle, noting the unshod pony prints he crossed. It was a little past noon when he saw the spirals of dust, three separate plumes not far from each other, and he headed the pinto for the nearest. Descending through a stand of bur oak, he reached a place where the land leveled out and he halted to watch six troopers racing in one direction, then in another. Four more soldiers appeared for a moment to ride off in still another direction.

They were plainly searching for something, but Fargo had seen no really fresh Cheyenne prints and he frowned as the small group of troopers continued to ride back and forth through the hills. Finally he saw the six-man detail halt and the other two groups ride toward it. A young lieutenant waved his sabre and the other troopers came to a halt and were again dispatched, this time in a single unit while the lieutenant took his six men north. Fargo wondered if the lieutenant was indulging in some form of practice exercise and discarded the thought. The troopers were riding with too much tension for that. Fargo, his lips pursed, turned the Ovaro and climbed higher into the hills, letting his practiced eyes scan every crevice and rise. He slowly surveyed the lines of bur oak and box elder and suddenly he caught the flicker of movement, up higher where the hills rose in a series of high rock formations grown over with trees.

He moved the pinto forward, up to higher ground, his eyes on the movement in the oaks at the high rocks. He moved upward in a wide arc, reached the rocks, and came in from the side and spied the flash of flaxen hair for an instant, then the long, slender form disappearing behind one of the tall rocks. He came out on the other side of the rock and was waiting on the narrow pathway as she came around to rein to a halt, surprise flooding her face. "What are you doing here?" she gasped.

"Satisfying my curiosity," Fargo said.

"About what?"

"About what those troopers are racing around to find," he said.

A hint of smugness touched her peaches-and-cream complexion, a faint blush of color. "I wanted to go riding alone and find a place to swim. Father insisted on sending an escort so I gave his escort the slip. I told you I wouldn't be a prisoner," Alison said.

"This time your pa was right. You shouldn't go riding alone. The Cheyenne are on a murdering rampage," Fargo said. "I'll take you down."

"No. I want a swim. I saw a pond up a hundred yards. You can stand watch," Alison said.

"Is that an order?".

"Yes," she sniffed.

"Go to hell, honey," he said evenly.

She blinked and brought her horse closer. "All right, no order. Dammit, you bring that out in me," she said.

"Doesn't take a hell of a lot to do it," Fargo remarked.

"You saying it's an inherited trait?" she asked and he shrugged. Her lips thinned. "I'm sorry, I don't want to be like him or sound like him. Forgive me."

"Why not?"

"But I still want a swim. Indulge me and stand guard. I won't be long," Alison said.

"Fifteen minutes," he said and she smiled and there was no triumph in it. He followed her to where a small, almost round, clear pond lay surrounded by rocks on all sides, a narrow passage leading through two of the rocks.

"I'll expect you to be a gentleman and not watch," Alison said.

"I said I'd stand guard. I didn't say anything about being a gentleman," Fargo told her.

She thought for a moment. "You will be," she said.

"What makes you so sure of that?" he questioned.

"If you watch me you can't stand guard," she said smugly and he laughed.

"One for you. Get moving," he said and turned the Ovaro behind the tallest of the rocks to where he found a ledge that let him survey the surrounding hills. He could hear her in the pond, splashing, diving and blowing air from her nostrils as she surfaced. The fifteen minutes were almost over, he calculated when the lone rider suddenly appeared on a ridge not too far away. The Cheyenne halted, peered across the hills, and Fargo backed the Ovaro into the passageway between the rocks. He backed up almost to the pond before he could turn around and he saw Alison near the edge, reaching out to take a towel from beside her clothes.

"You said you'd stand guard," she accused, still in the water.

"Shut up and get out of there," he hissed and her eyes grew wide as she brought the towel to her and wrapped it around herself as she came out of the water.

"Turn around so I can dress," she said.

"There's no time," he said. "Leave your things and follow me." He dropped from the saddle and led the horse into a crevice of a passage barely wide enough for the animal to fit. It didn't cut all the way through the rock and he halted, squeezing past the side of the horse to pause alongside Alison. "Stay here," he said and hurried back down the crevice to where it opened onto the pond and he dropped to one knee and waited. He felt more than heard Alison come up behind him. He waited, hardly breathing, silent as a lizard waiting for a toad. The Cheyenne may have turned and gone his way, he almost concluded as the minutes dragged on and then he heard the soft scrape of hoof against stone and he cursed silently.

The Indian came into view. He had been brought there by the pond and he let his pony drink as he slid from the animal's back. Fargo forced his hand down from the butt of the Colt. Maybe the Cheyenne was alone, but maybe he had friends nearby. If he did, a shot would bring them running. The Indian moved to climb back onto his pony as it finished drinking when Alison's horse, growing restless in the cramped crevice, shook its head vigorously. The rein chains rattled and Fargo saw the Cheyenne's head snap around, black eyes staring toward the crevice. He moved on light steps around the pony's rump and, drawing a tomahawk from the belt of his breechclout, he started toward the crevice.

Fargo paused to draw the throwing knife from its calf holster and emerged from the crevice to meet the bronzed figure. The Cheyenne was young, lithe, quick on his feet, Fargo saw at once as both men circled each other. Fargo decided against throwing the double-edged blade, for the moment at least, and was glad of his decision as he saw how quickly the brave moved to avoid his thrust with the knife. Fargo feinted again, came in with a downward thrust aimed at the arm holding the tomahawk. But again the Cheyenne deftly avoided the blow, circling to the left. He kept circling and feinted with a quick movement of his own and Fargo half ducked. He was off balance as the Indian lashed out with the tomahawk, a lightning-fast blow, and Fargo felt the edge of the short-handled ax scrape his shoulder as he pulled away. Instead of drawing back, the Cheyenne smashed into him with his shoulder lowered and Fargo felt himself stumbling sideways. He let himself fall, dropping to all fours as the tomahawk swiped at him, a flat, sidelong blow that passed just over his back.

Twisting with his hips, Fargo kicked out backward and the blow caught the buck in the abdomen and Fargo heard the breath rush from the man. The Indian fell back for an instant, enough for Fargo to twist again, fling himself onto the ground, and roll. He came up on his feet to see the Cheyenne charging him, tomahawk raised, less than a foot away. Even if he got his arm up to ward off the blow, the ax would smash into his forearm, Fargo knew. And trying to twist away might bring the tomahawk down into his back. He dropped to one knee, and holding the thin blade in the palm of his hand, flung it with an underhand motion, putting all the strength of his forearm into the toss. He was dropping flat on the ground as he saw the blade hurtle into the Indian, piercing the base of his throat. Fargo hit the ground as the Indian's feet struck him and the man fell forward across his prone body.

He rolled and came up on his feet to see the Cheyenne twisting, shuddering, stretched on his stomach, one hand pulling at the blade that had pierced him. The Indian managed to pull the blade out, only to release a gusher of red. He made gurgling, choking noises before he lay still, the blade falling from his hand and his life's blood still streaming from his throat. Fargo retrieved his throwing knife, wiped it clean on the grass, and returned it to the calf holster before he strode to the crevice where Alison waited, her blue-gray eyes wide. "Back your horse out," he said and she turned and squeezed past the mount and began to back the horse from the narrow crevice. Fargo waited, then went in, touched the Ovaro on the rump, and the horse backed itself out. Alison waited, the towel still wrapped around her but revealing one long, lovely thigh and very smooth, very round shoulders.

"Get dressed," he said and sent the pinto up the passageway where he halted beside the rocks outside. She joined him soon, astride the army mount, her face grave as she came alongside him.

"Thank you," she said. "I'm being a lot of trouble, it seems. I'm sorry."

"You are but there's a lot of trouble around. I'm not sure what it's all about yet. Let's get you back to those troopers," Fargo said.

"Yes." Alison nodded. "Lieutenant Elliot's a nice, sincere young man. A little slow, though. It was easy to give him the slip."

"Slow?" Fargo echoed. "How about trusting?" Alison let herself look chastened as he led the way down to where a single plume of dust still rose. When he reached the level land he came out just ahead of the smooth-faced young officer and his platoon. He saw a mixture of relief and anger sweep through the lieutenant's face as the officer spurred his horse forward.

"Dammit, Miss Carter . ..." Lieutenant Elliot bit out and then pulled back words.

"Don't stop," Fargo cut in. "Tell her what you think."

The lieutenant regained his composure somewhat. "If

anything had happened to you I'd have been shot, dereliction of duty or something," he said.

"I'm sorry," Alison said.

"Miss Carter's not going to be doing anything like that again, is she?" Fargo put in.

"No, she isn't," Alison said and the young officer turned to him.

"Thanks for bringing her back here safe," he said.,

"Not without trouble," Fargo said. "Cheyenne."

"Oh, God," Elliot groaned. "You're the man sent up by General Stanford, right?"

"News gets around fast." Fargo smiled.

"Always. You know that, I'm sure," Elliot said.

Fargo held the young officer's attention. "What do you know about Squad 4?" he asked.

"I command Squad 4 sometimes. We don't have enough officers to head every patrol so noncoms lead patrols sometimes. Corporal Reilly often takes out Squad 4," Elliot said. "They're all good men, most of them old-timer regulars."

Fargo nodded as he turned the lieutenant's answer over in his mind. It certainly didn't fit with what he had seen but he decided not to press further. Alison was giving him a long, speculative glance, he noticed, and the lieutenant cut into her thoughts. "Are you ready to go back, Miss Carter?" he asked.

"Yes, I am. So far as I'm concerned, none of this happened," Alison said.

"I'd appreciate that," Elliot said with obvious relief and Alison paused beside Fargo.

"Can we find a time to talk later?" she asked.

"I'll be up beneath the shadbush past the tents," he said and she nodded and fell in behind Lieutenant Elliot as he led his squad away. Fargo rode up into the high country again, checking the unshod prints, watching and exploring. It was nearing the end of the day when he began to nose down again. He'd almost reached the plain when he saw the squad of troopers riding by, a corporal in the lead. His eyes went to the pennant where the words SQUAD 4 leaped out at him. He watched the soldiers pass below and saw them go on in a wide circle that would eventually bring them back to the compound. He moved downhill, his mouth a thin line. He rode slowly and let the day draw to an end before he reached the stockade.

He tethered the pinto and walked into the general's office to find Alison there and the air crackling with tension. "Sorry, I'll come back," he said.

"No, stay. Father and I are finished," Alison said, her fists clenched at her sides.

"What is it you want, Fargo?" Carter asked impatiently.

"I want to know why I saw Squad 4 out patroling. I want to know why they're not being brought up on charges," Fargo said angrily.

"I questioned the troop. They told me the Cheyenne force was overwhelming. They had no choice but to run," Carter said.

"That's a crock of shit. I was there. I saw it," Fargo retorted.

"I believe my men. Subject closed," Carter said with arrogant imperiousness.

"Hell it is," Fargo shot back. "There are a lot of damn strange things going on here and I aim to dig deeper."

"Cheyenne raids are hardly strange occurrences," Carter said with a sneer.

"Troops who run are," Fargo said. "And it seems to me that an awful lot of womenfolk are being killed. How do you explain that?"

"Easily. The Cheyenne have waited for moments when men were away from their lands to make an easy strike," Carter said. "That's their cowardly way."

"I know the Cheyenne. That's not their way," Fargo said.

"It seems you're wrong," Carter said.

"Steer shit. I'm not wrong about Squad 4 and I'm not wrong about the Cheyenne ways. There's something damn strange going on," Fargo said.

"You've an overactive imagination, that's all. Go back to Miles Stanford and tell him the Cheyenne have been making trouble but I'm on top of it. My offer still stands to take Alison with you," the general said.

"My answer still stands," Fargo said, spinning on his heel and stalking out of the room. He climbed onto the Ovaro and sent the horse from the stockade at a fast gallop until he reached the shadbush on the low hill beyond the camp tents. He dismounted, a deep sigh escaping him. He relaxed enough to gnaw on a strip of cold jerky from his saddlebag. Carter was becoming more of an enigma. It was plain that he was all too willing to defend Squad 4, to accept their version of what had happened. Why? Because he hadn't the leadership to discipline them? Did he have so precarious a command of his own men? If so, he certainly hadn't the leadership to fight the Cheyenne. Was he simply the misfit General Stanford had called him, trying to hide his own incompetence?

Any of the explanations were possible yet none satisfied. They were all too simple and Carter seemed far too crafty. His explanation of why Squad 4 was escorting eight saloon girls was also too simple. If the corporal had volunteered such an escort because he was aware of Cheyenne trouble, why had he fled with his men when trouble appeared. It didn't fit. Nothing here fitted. Everything slid past everything else with a strange slipperiness. He broke off further thoughts as he saw the horse and rider coming up the hill toward him. When she reached him, Alison slid to the ground and came to sit beside him, the flaxen hair in the moonlight again giving her an ethereal quality.

"Tell me about Squad 4, everything that happened," she said.

"Everything?" he asked. "It won't be pretty."

"Everything," Alison said.

"Why? You think your father's lying?"

"I don't know, but I'm sure you're not," she said.

"A compliment?" Fargo asked mildly.

"I guess so," she said seriously. Fargo thought for a moment and decided to tell her all of it. She had a right to know. She was here smack in the middle of whatever was going to happen. When he finished, Alison held her hands to her face for a moment. "My God, those poor women. Oh, God, how awful," she murmured and there was pain in her face when she took her hands down.

"Now you heard it. What else have you heard?" Fargo questioned.

"I heard Father tell Lieutenant Elliot not to discuss anything with you and pass that order on to the men," Alison said.

"Fargo grunted. "I'm not surprised," he said.

"You know where the Cheyenne camp is. Why don't you press him to attack it?" she asked.

"That'd be a disaster. He'd lose damn near his whole command trying a direct attack on the Cheyenne camp. He's got to get the Cheyenne out in the open for a direct attack and I don't see him trying to do that," Fargo said. "Maybe he knows his men aren't fit to fight."

"Lieutenant Elliot seemed to think Squad 4 were all good men," she reminded him.

"So he did," Fargo agreed. "Something doesn't fit. Now, suppose you tell me why you had to come all the way out here to see the general?"

Alison let a weary sigh escape her. "When he and Mother divorced, there were papers he had to sign that would would let her use the money they had in the bank, money that she brought to the marriage from an inheritance. He never did sign them. He had himself assigned out here instead. For years and years, Mother's been trying to get him to sign those papers while she struggled to send me through school. She'd not been well the last year and she needs that money that's really hers."

"So you came to get him to sign the papers," Fargo said and Alison nodded. "You're not getting very far, I'll guess."

"That's right. He tells me he'll send them soon as I'm back home safe. He's weaseling, lying. I know it," she said. "I told him I'm not leaving without the signed papers. He said he'd ship me out under guard if he has to. That's where it stands at the moment."

"Can you force his hand through army channels? Embarrass him?"

"We tried that. He had too many friends in Washington," Alison said.

"What's your next move?" Fargo inquired.,

"I don't know. Wait him out, I thought, but I'm not sure I can do that. But he's underestimating me," Alison said and Fargo heard the anger harden her voice.

"What are you thinking about?" he questioned.

"I don't think I should tell you," she said.

Fargo smiled. "You wouldn't be thinking of having him sign at the end of a gun barrel, would you?" he remarked. His answer came in the flash of surprise that touched her eyes.

"What makes you think a thing like that?" she said and barely managed not to stammer.

"Because Daddy may underestimate you but I don't," he laughed and she glanced away. When she brought her gaze back to him her eyes were soft in a way he'd never seen before.

"How do you know me so well so quickly?" she asked.

"You cut trail you learn to see more than others do," he said.

"I'm glad you're here," she said and leaned forward and her lips were soft as a butterfly wing against his cheek and then she drew back at once and rose. "I've got to go," she said.

"On whose account?" he slid at her and she didn't answer as she climbed onto the horse. "Play the waiting game for now. Who knows what may happen," he told her.

"Advice?" she asked.

"Orders," he tossed back and saw her quick, bright smile as she rode off. Who knows what may happen, he repeated to himself but there was a grimness in the sound of it this time. Whatever happened, he had the definite feeling it wouldn't be good. He put his head back and let sleep come to him. He'd visit Willie Moccasin tomorrow, he promised himself.

# 5

He rose early and the sun was hardly clearing the distant hills when he rode upland to find the twisted Rocky Mountain maple and, beyond it, the half-hidden ravine. Willie Moccasin greeted him with a coffeepot in hand. "Didn't expect you at this hour," Willie said. "You're in luck. Just made fresh coffee."

"Sounds good," Fargo said and followed the wiry small form into the house and found Willie had also made some bannock with corn flour. They tasted delicious with the good, strong coffee. "I saw the chief they call Night Claw," Fargo said and Willie's leathered face hinted at surprise. "Bad man."

"Very bad," Willie agreed.

"I know where his camp is," Fargo said.

"Place to stay away from," Willie said.

"What have you found out for me?" Fargo asked, finishing his coffee.

"Nothing yet," Willie said and Fargo's brows raised a fraction. "Everyone afraid Night Claw has eyes and ears all over."

"How about someone outside the tribe?"

"Tonight I meet old friend. Maybe he will talk. You come back tomorrow," Willie said. "I must be careful. Night Claw finds out I help you I am dead man."

"I know that. You get to feeling nervous, you come into the compound," Fargo said.

"When do I come back to my place?"

"When Night Claw is finished."

Willie uttered a sardonic sound. "That Carter general never kill Night Claw."

"I may get him some help," Fargo said, rising to clasp hands with the little man. "I'll see you tomorrow," he said and Willie nodded gravely as Fargo left. The sun moving into the noon sky, Fargo rode through the hills, searching for Indian ponies, but the land was quiet and he made his way down from the hills and rode south. Poor Christy had told him they had all been saloon girls in Denville and he decided a visit there might be worthwhile. The day had slid into midafternoon when he reached the town, which turned out to be a small collection of worn buildings, mostly warehouse sheds, trading posts, and wagon supply merchants. The saloon was, as usual, in the center of town and he entered and ordered a bourbon from a middle-aged bartender with graying hair and a slightly sour face.

Fargo sipped his drink and let his gaze travel around the mostly empty saloon. He saw only two women in cheap, worn dresses. "I take it business picks up come dark," he remarked.

"Not likely," the bartender said. "Not till I get some more girls."

"What happened to the one you had?" Fargo asked.

"Goddamn army," the man spit out.

"The army?" Fargo frowned.

"That General Carter. He's been hurting business. Not just mine, either. Down at Leadville and High Rock, too," the bartender said.

"How?" Fargo frowned.

"He's been recruiting everyone's girls. Customer comes in for some fun and we can't give him any," the man said darkly. "Goddamn general's been hiring them all to service his troops, paying them extra bonuses."

"Never heard of that before," Fargo commented.

"Well, you have now. I've sent all the way into Colorado Territory for new girls. I'm waiting for them to get here. I just hope I can keep them," the man said.

"Good luck," Fargo said, paying for his drink and walking from the saloon, the frown inside him as he rode back the way he had come. Apparently General Carter was pioneering new twists in keeping his troops happy, Fargo mused, not an approach which Miles Stanford would approve. Why, Fargo pondered. Why not just let his men visit the town brothels in the time-honored custom of soldiers the world over? Was his discipline so poor he feared constant desertions? Fargo's thoughts went back to poor Christy as she lay in his arms.

She had said "army" when he'd asked where they had been going. He had thought she'd misunderstood him in her battered daze but she hadn't at all, and he felt a new surge of anger sweep through him. Carter had lied about why the troops was escorting the wagonful of women. His reasonable guess had been so much steer shit and his troopers had deserted the women he had hired, compounding their cowardice. Brutal irony, Fargo swore as he rode over the top of a hill and pulled the pinto to a halt. Just below him, a spring wagon, a topless, two-seat poor-man's surrey, rolled across the flatland with four young women in it.

Fargo spun the horse around and took a hill at a fast trot to come out almost alongside the wagon. The young women driving reined to a halt and Fargo's eyes swept the four occupants of the wagon. All had the telltale marks of their profession, too much makeup, too-tight dresses that let breasts spill partly over the neckline, faces that while still young enough, held a jaded weariness. "Afternoon, ladies," Fargo said. "What brings you out here all by yourselves?"

"Opportunity, big man," the one driving said cheerfully.

"Can't see much opportunity out here," Fargo said.

"We're not staying out here. We're on our way to the army compound," the young woman said. "I'm Tillie, this is Sally, Doris, and Honey," she introduced.

"General Carter send for you?" Fargo questioned.

"No, we've been hearing the army's hiring girls for good money so we decided to get some of the action," Tillie said.

"All you're going to get riding out here alone is scalped. The Cheyenne are on a rampage," Fargo said sternly and saw their eyes grow wide, fright flooding their faces.

"Jeez," Honey breathed. Her eyes went wildly across the hills.

"One wagon of girls on their way have already been killed," Fargo said.

"Jeez," Honey said again.

Fargo cast an eye skyward, where dusk was already starting to descend. "You'll never make the compound before dark. I think you ought to find a place to hole up," he said.

"Where? Hell, we don't know this country," Tillie said. "We're about lost now."

"I've a place you'll be safe," Fargo said and turned the Ovaro toward a slow rise and a pass into the hill country which the spring wagon could take. Night came in quickly and when a half-moon rose he found another passage the wagon could negotiate. He rode close to the wagon, beckoning the women to follow as he found one torturous passage after another. When the twisted maple finally appeared he guided the wagon down into the ravine where Willie came from the house at the sound, a yellow stream of light spearing out into the night. "Unexpected guests, Willie," Fargo said. "I'm sure you won't mind their staying the night."

"I'm not happy," Willie said.

"I've some news for you," Fargo told him as the women

climbed from the wagon with their bags. "It seems the general is hiring young women to satisfy his troopers. This way they don't have to go to town looking for pleasure."

Willie stared at him "You mean this, Fargo," he said and Fargo nodded. "Women suddenly very big thing," Willie said and it was Fargo's turn to stare back. "I have word about Night Claw," Willie said and Fargo was aware of the four saloon girls as they gathered around. "I should talk?" Willie asked.

"Go ahead. They're here. They're women. They're in the middle of it, like it or not," Fargo said.

"Night Claw is out to kill every woman settled on the land, every wife, sister, woman child. Night Claw believes no settler can exist without woman. Woman gives birth to man's children. She takes care of them and the home. Without his woman, no man could plow the land, plant the crops, settle his claim. He could not care for children and work the soil. Woman is the reason he can settle and live. Without woman, he will leave. No woman, no settler."

Fargo stared into space for a moment, the letter he had found in the house from Amos Hardy flaring inside him. "Night Claw may well be right, Willie," he said.

"He is bad man, like the river that cannot be moved from its course," Willie said.

"Then we'll have to find a way to stop him," Fargo said, his thoughts racing. Willie's information explained the Cheyenne attacks on women. It wasn't because they were simply choosing easy targets, as Carter had said. It was all part of the Cheyenne chief's grand plan and his thoughts went to the eight saloon girls so brutally attacked. They were simply unlucky victims of Night Claw's mad campaign, a madness rooted in a kind of truth. But the troopers' cowardice remained, still to be punished. Yet now he had more to talk to Carter about than punishment or recruiting saloon girls for his men. He turned to the four young women. "You'll stay here till I find a way to get you out safely," he said.

"Hell, we won't make any money here," Tillie objected.

"You won't make any dead, either," Fargo said.

"He's right, Tillie," one of the other women said. "We'll be staying."

Willie walked to the Ovaro with Fargo. "I'm not happy about this. The Cheyenne find out I'm hiding these women you know what happens to Willie Moccasin," he said.

"I'll get them out of here soon as I can," Fargo said as he climbed onto the horse and rode away at a canter. He rode through the night, halting only when the moon was high, to give himself a few hours' rest and when the new day dawned he continued on. He reached the compound and saw Alison come from her cabin as he dismounted.

"I went to the shadbush last night," she said. "I grew worried."

"Thanks, but I'm all right," Fargo said.

"You don't look all right. You look terribly grim."

"I've reasons," he said and strode into the office, aware that Alison entered with him. The general looked up from his desk, displeasure instant in his face.

"What brings this visit, Fargo?" he said coldly.

'I know what Night Claw's doing," Fargo said.

Carter's eyes narrowed. "Leave us alone, Alison," he said. "Leave the office now." Alison hesitated, then turned and left.

"Night Claw's not just hit-and-run raiding," Fargo said. "He's carrying out a plan to kill every woman on every farm, ranch, and settlement and you better damn well start doing something to stop him instead of recruiting saloon girls for your soldier boys."

"Where'd you hear about that?" Carter asked, his voice tensing.

"Word gets around."

"Keep your nose out of army affairs, Fargo. I know what I'm doing. You see, you haven't brought me any real news. We caught a Cheyenne who told us about Night Claw's plans, under persuasion, of course," Carter said.

"Then why haven't you brought in every family in the region?" Fargo questioned.

"Because they don't want to leave their homes to be burned down to the ground. They're expecting me to protect them and their homes."

"You can't do that, not with the bunch of cowards you have. Even if you had good men you don't have enough of them. The settlers are spread out too far. You need to send for more troops from General Stanford."

"I don't need Stanford's help," Carter exploded. "I've everything under control. I'm going to protect those good pioneer women."

"How?"

"That's army business," Carter shot back. "I know how these savages behave. Night Claw will grow tired of his plan and go on to something else."

"Meanwhile you're playing with people's lives because you're too damn conceited to ask for help," Fargo accused.

"I don't need help. I'm protecting those good women. Don't you worry about that. You can leave, now, mister," Carter said and Fargo strode from the office cursing silently. Alison was waiting outside.

"I heard. I left but I didn't go far," she said. "What are you going to do? Ride to Stanford and bring back more troops?"

"That'll take time, too much time. Maybe I can talk the settlers into coming into the compound. Then I'll go to Stanford," Fargo said. He paused when they were outside, his lake blue eyes searching her face before he decided to take the chance. "How angry at him are you?" he asked.

"Damn angry," Alison said tightly.

"Angry enough to spy on him?" Fargo queried.

"Yes," she said without hesitation. "Do I surprise you?"

"I'm not sure."

"He's my father. That's a biological fact. Other than that he's practically a stranger, one I don't like. What do you want me to do?" Alison said.

"Keep your eyes and ears open. He says he has his own plans for protecting the settler women. See if you can find out what they are," Fargo said. "Tell me anything you hear or see, I'll decide whether it's important."

She nodded and walked further with him as he led the Ovaro outside the stockade. "I know something now," she said. "But it's got to do with the saloon girls he's recruiting."

"Tell me," Fargo said.

"Two men are coming to see him tonight. I heard him talking to one of them about the saloon girls they've gotten for him. Apparently he's paying them off tonight," Alison said. "I know this isn't what's really important, now."

"It's not first place but I don't want to see another wagon of saloon girls massacred," Fargo said. "I'll check it out in my own way." He started to climb onto the Ovaro, paused, and pressed her arm. "And thanks," he said.

"Where do I find you if I have something more? Under the shadbush?"

"No. The shadbush is too close to the tents below. Go past it, straight up the hill till you come to a stand of bur oak," he said. "I'll be bedding down there whenever I can."

"I'll remember," she said. Fargo rode from the stockade area, striking out left along the land that bordered the high hills where he had come onto Amos Hardy's house. He found six others, spread out, some farmed well, others raising hogs and sheep. The settlers were friendly enough but, as with their type, stubborn and shortsighted.

"We appreciate you coming all the way out here to get us

to go down to the compound," a man named Corwin told him with his wife, a fourteen-year-old daughter and a four-year-old boy at his side. "But the general tells us he's taking care of things and we don't cotton to leaving our house and land."

Variations of the same refrain greeted Fargo at each place he stopped and when the day ended he made his way back to the compound. Carter had sold them well on the promise that he was going to keep the Cheyenne away. Just empty assurances from a conceited misfit, or did the general really have some plan, Fargo pondered as he brought the pinto to one side of the tents outside the stockade and halted in a thicket of box elder, where he could see the compound gate. He settled down to wait and watched the stillness come over the compound and the outside tents as the night deepened. He guessed it was almost ten o'clock when he spotted the two horsemen ride into the stockade and he straightened in the saddle. It was but a few minutes later when the two men rode out again and down the road leading south. He moved out of the boxelder and followed their path.

He hung back far enough not to be seen and his finely tuned hearing picked up their hoofbeats. He let almost a half hour go by before he drew the pinto to one side of the road, moved through the trees, and came abreast of the two men. He pulled the big Henry rifle from its saddle holster as he swung the horse down to the road and burst from the trees directly in front of the two riders. Both men started to reach for their guns and halted as they saw the rifle barrel trained on them. "Don't do anything we'll all regret," Fargo warned quietly. "I just want some talk and you can go your way."

"Talk about what?" one of the men said, apprehension in his sharp-nosed face.

"About the dance-hall girls you've been rounding up for the general," Fargo said.

"Nothin' to talk about. It's a job. We get the girls and he pays us for it," the man said.

"What'd he pay for tonight?" Fargo queried.

"A dozen girls, hired them out of fancy houses in Leadville and High Rock."

"You bringing them?"

"No, that's not our job. We hired two wagons with a driver for each. The general's sending a squad to escort the girls," the man said and Fargo made a wry sound as he thought about the last escort he'd witnessed.

"When?" he questioned.

"Tomorrow noon."

"Where?"

"The escort's picking them up north of High Rock."

"Where will you two be?" Fargo questioned.

"On our way south to Oldham. We've six more girls lined up there from the dance hall," the man said. "What the hell is this all about? Why the questions?"

"Curiosity," Fargo said and lowered the rifle though his finger remained on the trigger. "You can go on your way, now."

Exchanging confused glances, the two men shrugged at each other and moved their horses forward. Fargo watched them go on down the road before he turned and headed up into the hill country again. He rode back north, found a spot to bed down and slept till morning. He stayed in the hills, then, rode back to near where he had seen Squad 4 escorting the wagon, and dismounted beside a tall cottonwood to wait. From his vantage point he had a good view of the tree-covered hills in all directions and he scanned the land with narrowed eyes. But he saw nothing to alarm him in the mostly oak and box elder terrain, no movement that told him a line of silent horsemen were threading their way through the trees.

But he knew better than to be complacent. The Cheyenne could appear anytime, sudden and silent as the wind, and he knew they had not stopped prowling the hills, their hills. He could only hope the wagons would slip through in safety. The sun had passed the noon sky when he suddenly caught movement below in the distance. He watched it take shape and become the two wagons and the escorting troopers. He swung onto the pinto and began to move downhill until he could see the small caravan clearly. The young women were in two-horse Owensboro farm wagons and Fargo counted fourteen of them. The two men had said a dozen but two more had obviously joined in, Fargo grunted. His glance went to the escorting troopers, ten soldiers with the young-faced Lieutenant Elliot leading the squad. With another looming glance into the trees, Fargo sent the pinto downward and emerged onto the flatland a half-dozen yards ahead of the wagon and their escort. The lieutenant waved his men to a halt.

"You drew the assignment, it seems, Lieutenant," Fargo said.

"Yes, sir," Elliot said. "And I want to thank you again for the other morning."

"You can by telling me where you're taking these girls," Fargo said.

"Well, I'm not sure exactly. I may be taking them down to the compound area. I understand special tents are being set up for them," the lieutenant said.

"What do you mean you're not sure?" Fargo frowned.

"A trooper is supposed to meet us with final orders later on," Elliot said.

Fargo's frown remained. "If you may end up down at the compound, why go this way? This is the long way around through territory made for the Cheyenne."

Lieutenant Elliot half shrugged. "General's orders," he said. "Guess maybe he needs time to get their special tents put up."

"This doesn't make any damn sense," Fargo said and felt the uneasy feeling stirring inside him. "There are Cheyenne raiding parties all around here." The lieutenant shrugged again and Fargo speared him with a penetrating glance. "What if you're attacked, Lieutenant?" he asked. "What are your orders?"

He saw the lieutenant swallow and look uncomfortable. "We're not to lose valuable men engaging the Cheyenne," he said.

Fargo felt the uneasy feeling inside him turning into something made of incredulousness laced with spiraling horror. "Does that translate into running like hell?" he asked and the lieutenant's young face looked uncomfortable again.

"Our orders are not to engage the Cheyenne," he murmured and Fargo saw he had difficulty getting the words out.

"What about all these girls?" Fargo asked and Elliot glanced at the girls, who, Fargo saw, were listening intently. "Your orders are to desert them, aren't they?" Fargo pressed, "the way Squad 4 deserted the last wagonload?"

The young lieutenant didn't answer and his eyes looked down at his saddle horn. Fargo felt the fury churning inside him, fury made of disgust and horror and a sudden, numbing realization that was almost beyond belief. Only it was all too real, sickeningly, ravaging real and his hands were curled so tightly his knuckles were white. He wanted to whirl the Ovaro around and race to the compound but he knew he had something more important to do first. "Lieutenant, you escort these girl on this long way around through these hills and the Cheyenne will find you and attack. I'm changing your orders."

"Respectfully, sir, only the general can do that," Elliot said as he continued to look pained.

"You're right, but I'm going to see that you can't carry out those orders. I'm going to take these girls someplace safe," Fargo said and glanced at the two wagons, where every face was turned toward him. "You heard, ladies. You've an escort with orders not to fight when the Cheyenne attack, an escort with orders to desert you. Now, you can go on with that escort or come with me. Your scalps. Your choice."

"I'm not going to be deserted," one of the girls called out.

"Me neither," another said.

A full-bosomed, tall, black-haired young woman stood up to face Elliot. "Why have you got orders like that, soldier?" she asked.

Elliot's voice was barely audible as he answered. "I don't know, ma'am. Maybe the general knows he doesn't have enough men and doesn't want to lose any."

"Then why send a useless escort for us?" the woman asked.

Elliot shrugged and avoided her eyes. He was an honest young officer who believed in following orders yet found himself in a painful position, torn between duty and personal feelings. Fargo could have felt sorry for him but the burning rage inside him consumed all else but itself and he turned to the women again. "I take it that means you're coming with me, ladies," he said.

"Damn right," the chorus came and he glanced at the two wagon drivers.

"We'll go back with the lieutenant," one man said and Fargo's eyes went to Elliot.

"Your orders are to escort them, nothing else, right?" Fargo said and the lieutenant nodded. "Well your escort's been refused, now. You've no right to make them take your escort. You followed your orders. You're off the hook," Fargo said.

"I'll have to report this to the general," the young officer said, almost apologetically.

"You can also tell him I'll be down to see him," Fargo growled and Elliot nodded as he backed his mount away and two of the girls took the reins in the driver seat of each wagon. "This way," Fargo said with a wave of his arm and the two wagons began to roll forward after him. The lieutenant watched him lead the young women from the scene and finally wheeled his mount around to ride back to the stockade. Fargo, hoping his luck would hold before being spotted by the Cheyenne, led the two wagons higher into the hills, through passages just barely wide enough for them to fit. The day was beginning to draw toward an end when he brought his new charges into the ravine.

The four girls from the spring wagon came forward and Willie rushed from his house. "Brought you some more guests, Willie," Fargo said and halted to meet Willie's angry frown.

"You trying to get me killed, Fargo?" the small man asked.

"No, trying to keep these young ladies alive," Fargo said. "Nobody saw us come here and I couldn't think of anywhere else with enough room. I'll be back for them."

"I heard that before," Willie muttered and Fargo brought the Ovaro alongside the wagons.

"What's your name, big man?" the tall, black-haired young woman asked.

"Fargo . . . Skye Fargo."

"I'm thinking we owe you one, Fargo," she said.

"Right now you owe Willie Moccasin. His bark is worse than his bite. You do what he says until I get back," Fargo told them.

"We'll be properly grateful to him," one of the girls called out.

"Just remember he's not as young as he used to be," Fargo grinned as he sent the Ovaro from the ravine where his face again became dark with fury. The day still clung to the land and he rode hard, taking shortcuts through thick, brambly terrain and down steep slopes. The terrible conviction inside him had grown, no longer able to be denied, and there were so many things suddenly with new explanations. Inside, he was both sick and enraged. Night had just settled in when he reached the stockade and skidded the Ovaro to a halt.

He marched into the general's office and heard Alison's voice raised in angry argument. She broke off as he entered and Carter snapped to his feet, his face instantly darkening in icy fury. "You son of a bitch. I didn't think you'd have the nerve to show yourself here. How dare you interfere with what I'm doing for my men?" Carter accused.

"You're not doing anything for your men, you rotten bastard," Fargo flung back and heard Alison's gasp. "I know what you're really doing with those saloon girls. You didn't bring them here to service your men. You brought them to toss to Night Claw."

Carter's eyes narrowed. "I don't know what you're talking about," he said.

"The hell you don't. That's your plan to protect the settler women. You figure Night Claw will think these are settler womenfolk and you're probably right there. You also expect he'll be satisfied at what he's doing and you'll keep tossing him more saloon girls so he'll stay away from the settler women."

Alison's voice cut in. "Is that right? Is that what you're doing?" she asked, disbelief in her tone.

"Mind your own business and stay out of this," the general said, the veins throbbing in his left temple.

"Oh, God, it is true," Alison gasped in shock.

"You're damn right it's true. He provides the girls with an escort so Night Claw will be sure to think they're settler women and orders his men to desert them at the first attack," Fargo said.

"And it's working, too. There's hasn't been an attack on the good womenfolk since I started this," Carter said.

"You crazy, rotten bastard," Fargo said.

"I'd expect that from someone such as you, a man with few values. Those settler wives, sisters, and daughters, are all fine, decent, God-fearing, respectable women, the kind we need to settle this land. What are these others? Whores, that's what. Worthless, low-down, drinking whores, no better than alley cats. Most of them end up killed, anyway. They're worthless pieces of humanity. A dozen of them aren't worth one of those fine, hardworking, respectable women."

"My God, my God, I can't believe what I'm hearing," Alison said, her voice hollow.

Fargo slammed the side of his fist on the desk. "Who the hell do you think you are, Carter?" he roared. "Who gave you the right to decide who's worth living and who isn't? Who made you judge and jury of other people's lives? You're no different that Night Claw. You're two of a kind, both arrogant, twisted madmen, one wearing a loincloth, the other a uniform."

Carter's mouth trembled in barely contained fury. "What's you do with the damn girls, Fargo?" he demanded.

"You're not going to find out," Fargo said.

Carter spit out a curse as he clapped his hands. Three troopers stepped from an adjoining room, carbines in hand. "Put this man in the guardhouse," the general ordered. Fargo calculated his chances if he went for his revolver. They were worse than poor, the three carbines trained on him, and he stayed unmoving as the troopers surrounded him, one taking the Colt from its holster. "You'll rot in there until you tell me where those damn whores are, Fargo," Carter shouted as Fargo was led away.

It wasn't far to the guardhouse, which was at the rear of the stockade. The troopers put him inside a small, barred cell with a desk and a chair outside the bars. Fargo lowered himself onto a narrow cot inside the cell and glanced at the small, high barred window. One of the troopers paused at the doors as they started to leave. "There'll be two of us on guard just outside. You need anything you holler and we'll hear you," the soldier said and Fargo saw the unhappy expression cross his face. "I was with Lieutenant Elliot when you brought the general's daughter back. We'd all have been in big trouble if anything had happened to her. I'm sorry about all this, mister. The general's a strange man but I just follow orders," the soldier said.

"That's your job, soldier. No hard feelings," Fargo said and the man left still looking unhappy. As the door closed behind him, Fargo's hand moved down to the calf holster with the thin blade tucked inside it. He smiled, glad the soldiers had stupidly assumed the Colt was his only weapon. But he'd have to bide his time till the night was late and the camp asleep. He stretched out on the cot and closed his eyes. Until then, he'd make the most of the general's hospitality.

# 6

He guessed it was late but still before midnight when he snapped awake at the sound of the guardhouse door opening. He swung from the cot to see one of the troopers letting Alison into the room and then closing the door after her. Alison was at the cell bars in three quick strides. "What are you doing here?" Fargo asked in surprise.

"I told them my father sent me to question you, thinking maybe I could convince you to talk," she said. She reached down inside the long-sleeved shirt she wore and the Colt was in her hand when it came back out.

"How'd you get that?" Fargo frowned.

"In the desk in Father's office," she said a little smugly as she handed him the gun. "Now you can get out of here."

"No, not like this. They'll know you brought me the gun," Fargo said.

"I don't care anymore, not after what I heard tonight. You were right. He's a madman," Alison said.

"And I wouldn't trust what he'd do to you, even if you are his daughter, and I can't take you with me, not yet," Fargo said. "Besides, you'll be more valuable to me moving around freely, not locked in your quarters."

"But you've got to get out of here," Alison said.

"I will but we have to keep your nose clean," Fargo said. "Put the Colt away for now and give it to me when we're outside."

"How are *we* going to be outside?" Alison questioned.

Fargo grinned as he reached down and drew the thin, double-edged knife from its calf holster. "One of us is escaping and one of us is going to be a hostage. Turn around," he said and when Alison turned, her back against the bars, he reached out and pressed the knife to her throat. "Down this end," he said, moving a half-dozen feet from the cell door. "Now call the guards. Be scared."

She screamed the word twice and the guardhouse door burst open and two of the troopers entered, carbines in hand. They stopped as they saw Alison with the knife to her throat. "Do as he says, please," Alison begged and Fargo smiled inwardly. She was putting on a good performance.

"Close the door," Fargo said and one of the guards kicked the door shut. "Now drop the guns," Fargo said.

The trooper who'd spoken to him earlier let his rifle drop to the floor with unhappy reluctance. "I didn't think you'd do anything like this, mister," he said.

"Desperate men do desperate things," Fargo said. "Now open the cell door." The man moved toward the bars. "Now, dammit, before my hand slips," Fargo rasped and the trooper used the key to unlock the cell. "Get back," Fargo said as he moved toward the open cell door, still holding Alison through the bars, keeping the knifepoint against her throat as he reached the door and stepped out of the cell. Putting his arm around her waist, now, he laid the edge of the knife against her throat as he moved to the side. "Get in the cell, both of you," he ordered and the two men obeyed. He kicked the cell door and it slammed shut. Pausing only to yank the key out, he pushed Alison in front of him from the guardhouse and then he was outside, running with her across the dark, sleeping compound.

"It worked," she breathed.

"I'm out and you're in the clear. You tell the general you came to see me on an impulse and you realize now it was a mistake," Fargo told her as they reached the stables where he found the Ovaro still saddled in one of the stalls. "I'll take the Colt now," he said. "Your father will assume I did just what you did, sneaked in and took it." He paused and reached out and pulled her to him. He felt the softness of her full breasts against him. She didn't protest and he let his mouth cover hers for a brief moment. "Thanks for what you tried to do," he said, pulling back. "You're turning out to be the only pleasant surprise in this whole damn thing."

"I'm glad for that," she said and this time it was her lips that came forward, a sweetness to her, and she pulled back reluctantly. "Will I look for you beyond the shadbush?" she asked.

"No, you stay quiet here. Your pa may have someone keeping an eye on you for the next few days," Fargo said.

"That would be like him," Alison said with distain.

"I'll contact you," he said. "I'll find a way." She walked part of the way with him as he led the Ovaro to the stockade door that was, with arrogance, left open, he noted. He swung onto the horse and rode slowly into the open, knowing that her eyes followed him until the night swallowed him up. He circled the army tents outside the compound, leaving plenty of room, and made his way north and into the hills. He found a spot to bed down in a clump of hackberry and when the morning came he rode the high country slowly, surveying the terrain and smiled when the squad of troopers came into sight below.

He picked out Lieutenant Elliot in the lead and counted fifteen troopers with him. The lieutenant paused often to scan the hills and then went on again and Fargo smiled. The lieutenant had been sent out to try and find the two wagons with the saloon girls and he was following a cross-pattern in his search. But he was far from the mark and Fargo moved through the trees and rode higher into the hills, not at all certain that the lieutenant wasn't just going through the motions. Fargo sent the pinto through the trees just to take no chances and it was midday when he rode into the ravine and reined to a halt.

An air of almost domesticity had enveloped the place, with dresses and bloomers hanging on makeshift clotheslines strung from the wagons to the trees. The women came forward as Fargo dismounted, along with Willie, who wore an expression of pained patience. "We were getting worried," the tall, black-haired woman said.

"Can't blame you," Fargo said.

"I'm Rita, by the way," the woman said. "What happens to us now?"

"Been thinking hard about that," Fargo said. "As I see it, if you want to stay alive you're going to have to fight, on your own."

"What about the damn army?" one of the others called out.

"General Carter only wants you as fodder to toss at the Cheyenne."

"The son of a bitch," Tillie said.

"He has his squads out trying to find you. If he does find you he can't let you stay alive to talk about what he wanted to do with you. He intended to toss you to Night Claw all along, now he has to," Fargo said.

"What do we do, sneak out of here at night?" Rita asked.

"You can't do it by night. Too much territory to cover. You'll be caught in the open when day comes, either by the general's troops or by the Cheyenne."

"We can't camp here forever," Rita said.

"No, you're right because Night Claw will find you here sooner or later," Fargo agreed. "He's still the main player. He's the one who is out to kill every woman he can find. You're going to have to face him and win, kill him before he kills you."

"You crazy, Fargo? There's no way we can fight a Cheyenne chief and his damn warriors," Rita said.

"We'll find a way. It's your only chance. We stop Night Claw and I'll see to the good general," Fargo said. Willie Moccasin regarded him with a speculative stare.

"Fargo not one for empty talk. He has a plan," the wiry little man pronounced.

"Sort of," Fargo smiled, sweeping the woman with a long glance. "How many of you know how to use a rifle?" he asked. "How many of you can hit something with one?" Three of the eighteen women raised their hands. "The rest of you are going to get a crash course," he said. "I'll be back by tomorrow night."

"You know we'll be waiting," Rita said as Fargo swung onto the Ovaro and rode from the ravine. He rode hard down from the hill country, slowing only to circle Lieutenant Elliot and his troopers as they were still searching the low hills. Cheyenne scouts were somewhere watching the patrol, Fargo was certain, waiting to see if they were meeting another wagon filled with women. He gave the patrol a wide circle as he continued on and night fell before he reached the compound. The army tents outside the stockade had already grown quiet when he arrived. He dismounted and led the horse down the long slope to the rear of the stockade.

He waited in the black shadows for another hour to pass, then left the pinto with its reins tied to the ground and proceeded on foot in a crouch. He paused at the open stockade gate, pressed himself against the tall wood walls, and swept the compound with his eyes. One barracks still had a light burning inside but that flicked out as he watched. He waited another fifteen minutes and then, moving with his back against the stockade wall, made his way toward the cabins adjoining the general's quarters. Only when he was opposite the cabin where Alison was quartered did he dash across the open space inside the compound, moving in silent, quick steps to reach the cabin. His hand clasped around the doorknob, he opened the door just enough for him to slip through the cabin. The faint moonlight filtered through the window to crawl across the bed with the flaxen-haired form atop it.

He crossed the floor in three long strides and gently put one hand over Alison's mouth. He held it there as she came awake, fright in her eyes until she recognized the figure at her bedside. He drew his hand back and she sat up, a filmy white nightgown barely concealing the full swell of her breasts, and her arms went around his waist. "You're mad, coming here like this," she said.

"I wish I could stay," he said.

"I wish you could, too," Alison said, her voice very soft.

"Put something on. I need your help," he said and she swung from the bed, turning her back on him as she slipped the nightgown off and a blue shirt on, letting him catch only a glimpse of a smooth, beautifully curved back and long legs. She wrapped a skirt around the shirt and slipped into sandals.

"Ready," she said.

"You happen to see where the extra rifles are stored?" Fargo asked as they left the cabin and he paused outside to scan the silent compound.

"Yes, in a shed at the rear of the compound," she said and he let her lead the way to the square board shed. The door was unlocked. He stepped inside and left the door open to let in the pale light of the moon. He saw a typical arms storage shed, some hundred or so extra rifles standing in rows on wooden racks, and one wall piled high with boxes of ammunition. Fargo began to remove twenty-five of the rifles, taking them from inside the rows so anyone glancing in wouldn't see a gap of missing guns. He worked as quickly as he could and stay silent and when the rifles were on the floor he added a dozen boxes of the ammunition.

"We can't carry this out the front gate and around to my horse. We'd have to make half a dozen trips and somebody could spot us at any time, look out a window, wake up in one of the outside tents, and see us . . . any damn thing that's blow it all up in our faces."

"So what do we do?"

"We carry this stuff to the rear of the stockade, against the fence. Let's go," he said, taking a half-dozen of the rifles in his arms. Alison followed with as many as she could carry and he led the way along the sides of the stockade, staying in the deepest night shadows, until he set everything down against the rear fence. Another six trips brought the last of the ammunition boxes to the fence. Fargo turned to Alison. "How are you at tying knots?" he asked.

"Good enough," she said.

"I'll be tossing a lariat over the top of the fence to you. When you get to the other end, tie a bundle of the rifles together. Give the lariat two jerks when you've finished and I'll do the rest until I toss the lariat back to you."

Alison nodded and Fargo left her by the rear wall and moved away in a crouching lope. She reached the stockade gate and went out to the other side of the fence. When he reached the Ovaro he took the lariat and sent one end of it flying up and over the top of the stockade and in a moment he felt Alison take hold of it. He waited while she tied a bundle of rifles on the other side of the fence. Finally when he felt the two, short snaps of the rope he began to pull on the lariat. He felt the weight on the other end of the rope as it rose to the top of the stockade. When he saw the bundle of rifles he stopped pulling, uncurled another length of the lariat, and tossed it upward. It took him three tries before he caught the rope around the pointed top of one of the stockade posts. Using the second length of rope in block-and-tackle fashion, he lowered the rifles to the ground on his side of the stockade. He untied them and tossed the end of the lariat over the top of the stockade again and felt Alison catch hold of it.

The careful, tedious operation took far longer than he had wanted and dawn was beginning to edge the distant sky when he had the last box of ammunition on the ground beside him. Hurrying, he tied the rifles and the ammunition boxes to the Ovaro and used the rest of the lariat to form a makeshift double-rigged saddle. There was no time to go back to Alison but he knew she'd understand and as he rode away he thought he detected a slender figure at the edge of the stockade gate. The new dawn came as he rode upward and paused often to let the horse rest. It was midday when he saw Lieutenant Elliot and his platoon below, once again scouring the hills to find the saloon girls.

He watched the Lieutenant ride off westward and then he sent the Ovaro higher into the hills. He reached a stand of bur oak when he glimpsed the distant line of near-naked horsemen and took refuge in the oaks. They rode far more slowly then the lieutenant's platoon but it was obvious that they were searching, also, halting frequently to scan the terrain below. He watched them break into two groups and explore in different directions and join again further down in the hills. They disappeared from sight finally and Fargo moved out of the oaks and continued on his way. He fought off the toll of sleeplessness and reached the ravine a little before the day ended. The women and Willie Moccasin helped unload the rifles and the ammunition. "We start in the morning," Fargo said. "Right now I need a good night's sleep."

Willie brought him a bowl of rich corn soup and after finishing it Fargo took his bedroll to the side of the ravine, unsaddled the Ovaro, and stretched out in the night, letting the warm wind blow over his nakedness. Sleep came quickly and he woke only when the new sun made its way into the ravine. He washed with his canteen, dressed, and found the women finishing coffee in a half-circle around Willie's house. Willie emerged with a tin cup of the hot brew for Fargo who sipped as he untied the rifles and opened the ammunition boxes. "We'll go down to the end of the ravine," he told the women. "Each of you take a rifle. Willie will show you how to load and hold it while I get some targets ready."

He went ahead down to the far end of the ravine and set up a line of wide twigs and bits of broken branches. "On your stomachs," he said to the women as they arrived. "There's one target for each of you. Take aim and start firing. Stop when you hit yours." He stepped back and watched as the women began to fire their rifles and was pleasantly surprised at how quickly they hit their targets. He set up another line of broken branches and had them fire again. After two more sets of targets he was happily surprised to see that, for the most part, they were natural shots. He next rigged up his lariat to run downward from one tree branch to another. With Willie's help, a piece of flat wood was tied to the rope with a metal ring and attached to another length of lariat which, when pulled, brought the piece of wood moving quickly down the long length of lariat to make a moving target.

This time he had the women fire singly as Willie yanked on the target line and this time the results were not as encouraging. "It's only the first time you've shot at a moving target," Fargo told them afterward. "You're going to keep doing it all day every day for the next two days. Just remember, don't shoot directly at the target. Shoot a fraction of an inch in front of it so your bullet and the target reach the same spot at the same time. Willie will be in charge till I get back."

"What happens when we finish practicing, Fargo?" Rita asked.

"We go out to meet Night Claw," Fargo said and heard

the small murmur of uncertainty move through the women. "We don't want him finding you. That'll give him all the advantages. We want to use the only two things that can work for you, surprise and marksmanship. I'll fill in the details later. Meanwhile you keep practicing till you can shoot straight."

Willie walked to the Ovaro with him and spoke in a hushed voice. "It can't work, even if they all become crack shots, which they won't," Willie said. "They can't stand off a full Cheyenne attack."

"I know that," Fargo said and Willie grunted.

"Figured you would. So what are you planning?"

"First, they can do real damage by surprising them. Then I have to have help ready," Fargo said.

"Help from where? Carter won't help. He wants Night Claw to have them."

"Yes, but maybe there's a way."

Willie gave him a long, speculative look. "You sound like a man hanging on to the end of a long rope," he said.

"Guess I am, old friend, a rope called conscience, the better side of human nature," Fargo said.

Willie sniffed. "Good luck."

Fargo climbed into the saddle and walked the Ovaro forward. "Work with them, Willie," he said and went into a trot. He rode through the day, losing time on three different occasions when he had to hide from Cheyenne scouting parties. The night was deep when he reached the stockade and tethered the Ovaro to a low branch in a cluster of hackberry. Once again, the stockade entrance was open. Carter was a complete egotist as well as stupid, Fargo muttered to himself as he slipped into the stockade and edged his way along the walls to reach Alison's cabin. He disliked involving her again but he had no choice. He'd make it up to her. He'd see that she got those papers signed.

He halted at the door of the cabin, tried the knob, and

found it open. Slipping inside, his eyes went to the bed across the room. It was empty. Alison wasn't in the cabin and the bed hadn't been slept in. His eyes grew hard as the sudden apprehension flared inside him. Had something gone wrong? Had she made a mistake in anger? It was all too possible. She'd enjoy cutting her father down. Or had it been something else, entirely beyond her? Fargo moved from the cabin and edged his way toward the guardhouse to drop to one knee as he saw the two troopers outside the door. A host of emotions churned through him but surprise wasn't among them. It would be entirely in character for the general to put his own daughter in the guardhouse. Fargo's eyes bored into the two troopers as he was already forming plans on how to free Alison. But as his eyes stayed on the two troopers he suddenly realized something else.

They weren't simply standing guard in the usual fashion. They were both tense, fully alert, their eyes peering into the darkness. Fargo let his gaze move from the two troopers to probe the deep shadows along the opposite wall of the stockade. It took him minutes until he made out the darker shadows spaced a dozen feet apart, troopers waiting, watching the guardhouse. Fargo's smile was made of ice as he backed away, staying in his own deep shadows. He crept back past Alison's cabin to the general's quarters, where a lamp burned inside. He closed one hand around the doorknob and turned, ever so slowly. The door opened, the faint click instantly muffled by his other hand and he heard the voices from the general's office, Alison's first.

"How long are you going to keep this up?" she said.

"Every night, as long as I have to," Fargo heard Carter reply and he crept forward until he was able to see into the office through the partly open door.

"He won't come here. Why should he?" Alison said.

"To get you to help him again," Carter said.

"You're all wrong," Alison said.

"Stop lying," the general snapped. "He'll come, find you're not in your quarters, and put two and two together and go to get you out of the guardhouse. Then we'll have him."

"Close but no cigar," Fargo said, stepping into the room with the Colt in hand and Carter spun in astonishment. Alison started to rise from the chair and fell back and Fargo saw her hands were tied behind her to the chair. Carter was still staring at him, his mouth hanging open. "Untie her," Fargo said, stepping closer, his finger on the trigger of the Colt. "I'd hate to shoot a man in front of his daughter but I'll make an exception in your case."

Carter pulled his jaw shut, stepped behind Alison, and untied her hands. "You'll never get away with this, Fargo," he said.

"Guess again," Fargo said. "Now we'll stay right here while Alison goes to the stable and gets her mount."

"The troopers on guard will stop her," Carter said and Fargo's smile was chiding.

"No. They'll watch her and wonder but they won't stop her. I'm betting they have no orders to stop her," Fargo said and his answer was in the dark red of the general's furious face. Alison hurried from the room and Fargo kept his Colt on Carter.

"You'll hang for this, Fargo," Carter rasped.

"Maybe, but not tonight," Fargo said.

"You've put the lives of every decent settler woman in jeopardy," Carter hissed.

"You did that when you began your madman's idea of sacrificing saloon girls to Night Claw instead of asking Miles Stanford for more troops," Fargo said.

"It was working until you poked your face into it," Carter said. "I had that savage doing things my way."

"That's real funny," Fargo said.

"What is?"

"You calling Night Claw a savage. He's out to kill women following his own logic. Terrible as that may be, he's not playing God about it. He's not deciding who's got more right to live. You're the real savage here, Carter," Fargo said. He heard the sound at the door and half turned to see Alison there.

"I'm ready," she said and he nodded and turned to go to her. He spun as the sound came from behind him, a roar of fury, and he saw Carter at his desk drawer, yanking it open and raising the army standard-issue Remington .44. Fargo fired, the reaction automatic, just as Alison's half-scream reached him. "No!" she cried out and her hand hit his arm and he saw the bullet go past Carter into the wall. Carter half-fell behind the desk as he ducked away and Fargo ran, Alison pulling him with her.

They were out the door as Carter regained his feet and fired a shot wide of the mark. Fargo vaulted onto the army mount and reached down and swung Alison on behind him. Her arms clasped around his waist, he sent the horse racing out of the stockade as Carter came from his quarters, shouting and firing. "After them, dammit. Shoot him," Carter yelled but Fargo had the horse rounding the edge of the gate and racing to where he'd left the Ovaro. He reined to a halt at the horse, leaned over, and transferred himself as Alison took the reins of the army mount. The sounds of horses being saddled and mounted came from the other side of the stockade and Fargo hurried uphill through the stand of oak.

"They'll ride around hoping to get lucky but they won't find us in the night," Fargo said and cut a curving path through the trees to finally halt in a deep thicket. He waited there, Alison beside him, and listened to the distant sounds of the troopers riding aimlessly through the hills until they finally broke off their search. He moved from the thicket and let the horses walk their way uphill.

"I'm sorry about what happened back there, my hitting your arm," Alison said. "It was automatic, a reflex action. I couldn't help myself. I didn't want you to shoot him."

"Blood has its bonds. I understood," he said and continued on to the high plain, circled the edge of it, and rode into the high country again. The moon had disappeared beyond the distant hills when he reined to a halt in a small alcove bracketed by rock at one side and red cedar at the other. He had passed the spot before and knew the surrounding land and felt comfortable. "We'll sleep here. No need for hurrying, now," he said.

Alison came to him after unsaddling her horse. "You couldn't have known he was holding me prisoner. Why'd you come?" she asked.

"To get your help again," he said. "But we'll talk about that come morning. Tell me what happened to make him think you'd helped me."

"The missing rifles," Alison said. "One of the supply sergeants making a routine inspection found them gone. I denied any part of it, of course, but he didn't believe me."

"Damn," Fargo swore.

"He realized you had to take them the night you escaped by holding me hostage but you couldn't have done it alone."

"Which meant you weren't exactly a hostage," Fargo grunted and cursed the problems caused by the unexpected as he laid down a blanket for Alison.

"Thanks. All my things are back at the compound," she said. "I can't even change to wash things."

"We'll find a change for you. Now get some sleep. I expect you haven't been getting too much of that the last few days," he said.

"You imagine right," she said and stretched out on the blanket. He lay down beside her and watched her fall asleep almost instantly, her full breasts rising and falling under her shirt with steady regularity. He lay awake a little longer. His plans had been shattered. He'd have to form new ones to accomplish the same goal and he finally slept with that realization in mind.

# 7

The morning sun was full in the sky before he woke. Casting an eye on Alison, who lay on her side, flaxen hair not unlike a cluster of yellow sunflowers, he stepped past the rocks to where the small lake sparkled in the morning sun. Soon Alison came to stand beside him. "Thought you'd like a swim and a bath," he said.

"God, yes," she breathed and he walked the hundred yards to the lake, where just beyond the shoreline, a long stretch of soft mountain fern moss formed a deep carpet. Alison halted at the edge of the lake and began to unbutton her shirt.

"You're full of surprises," Fargo commented and she let the blond eyebrows lift in question. "You're not insisting I turn around," he said.

"I don't want you to turn around," she said quietly and shed the shirt, then her skirt and the slip under it to stand beautifully naked before him. He felt his breath draw in at the loveliness of her. The peaches-and-cream complexion in her face echoed in the glowing skin of her body and he took in beautifully rounded, wide shoulders and full breasts that seemed to shimmer with both delicacy and sensuousness, a long curve to them, full at the cups with very pink nipples that stood firmly erect against equally pink, small areolas. Her rib cage was strong and deep and her wide hips seemed narrower than they were. She had long, beautifully curved legs with gorgeous thighs and just above them a blond nap that curled outward with its own delicacy.

He was still staring at the magnificent beauty of her, the peaches-and-cream of her imparting a virginal quality that was somehow terribly sensual and beckoning. She turned and walked into the water, a flat, firm rear hardly moving when she halted, in just over her nap, to look back at him. "Aren't you going to join me?" she asked.

"Best idea I've heard in a long time," he said as his fingers began undoing buttons. She had sunk under the surface for a moment to come up again, standing in water up to her waist. The glistening drops gave her a new, shimmering beauty and he saw her eyes on him as he stepped into the lake. She came to him, her smooth-wet skin pressed against him, her lips finding his, quivering, opening, pulling, then moving away as she whirled and dove and surfaced only to dive again, playful and graceful as an otter. He dived under the surface, also, letting the water clean the road dust from his body, and suddenly she came up behind him and pressed her breasts into his back for a brief instant and then swam away.

She came up a half-dozen feet away and pointed to a ground of small trees at the edge of the carpet of fern moss. "Aren't those wild plum trees?" she asked and he nodded. She struck out for the shore, sprang from the water, and half ran to the trees, her breasts swaying together in a beautiful rhythm and she was on her second plum when he joined her and sank down on the moss. He caught the plum she tossed him as he swept her loveliness with his eyes. She was entirely changed, no reticence, no prim properness, no haughtiness. Instead she was an unabashed child of nature, yet with a very womanly sensuousness to her. She lay back, her breasts rising upward, nipples touched by tiny droplets of water still quivering on their pinkness. He leaned forward and licked one of the droplets from the very tip, then another.

"Oh, God," Alison breathed and he felt her body quiver and then her arms were reaching up, circling his neck. His mouth closed around one smooth breast, the tiny tip touching inside his and his hand caressing the softness of her other breast. "Mmmmmm, oh . . . mmmmmm," Alison murmured as he caressed the very light pink areola with his tongue, circling the outer perimeter of it as he felt Alison's hips rise and fall back again. He took his mouth from the smooth breast and brought it to her lips. Her tongue darted forward, quick, urgent little motions as his hand caressed the full breasts, gently rubbing across each light pink tip. "Aaaaah, aaaaah . . . oh, yes, yes," Alison murmured and her hands moved up and down his body, pressing hard, then growing light, then pressing again.

He let his lips move down the peaches-and-cream skin again, across her breasts, and he traced a path down over the space between her ribs, down further, nibbling, moving over her abdomen, pausing at the tiny indentation. Alison clasped his head and pressed his face into her abdomen. He moved lower, burying his face into the blond nap, feeling the fiber-soft tendrils against his face, a strangely exciting touch. He held against the little rise of her Venus mound, and as he pressed down harder he felt Alison's thighs fall open and come together again and fall open once more. His hand curled around the sweet portal and he felt the moistness of her inner thighs. "Oh, God, oh, God . . . yes, please, oh please," Alison murmured and again her hips rose and came down and Fargo's hand moved gently, touching the tender wetness at the very tip of her pulsating portal and Alison's scream rose instantly.

He moved deeper, slowly caressing her, and Alison was crying out little murmuring sounds under the warm sun and her torso half twisted from side to side, slow, undulating motions as he caressed deeper. The delicate peaches-and-cream color of her skin had changed, he saw, her body now a light pink, and he moved himself over her, the erect firmness coming down onto her blond nap. "Aaaaaiii . . ." Alison half screamed, drawing herself back and offering her waiting warmth to him. He slid into her, a slow, sweet incursion, and he felt her flowing around him, roscid embrace. Alison's long thighs were around him and she moved with him, languorous exercises in absolute pleasure as he joined with her in the total immersion of the senses.

She pulled his face down to her breasts as she rose and thrust with him, back and forth, the body savoring itself, crying out in the language of the senses. He lifted his face to take in the utter beauty of her long body, all delicate pink smoothness under the sun, lifting and arching with him, adding consummate loveliness to consummate wanting. "Oh, yes, oh, God, it . . . it . . . it's happening," he heard her cry out, a moment of panic and unbearable ecstasy combining in her voice, and he felt her trembling in his embrace and there was no holding back for either of them. The vast, groaning sound was his own, he realized as she clung hard against him, pumping frantically now, crying out gasps of sounds, and suddenly the world was contained in two bodies, in a single, glorious moment that was without end and yet ended without mercy.

He lay with her and heard her small half-sobbing sounds. "Too soon, too soon," she murmured. "Too quick, too little." He held her as she quivered, finally lying still, and he pulled his face against her breasts, one pink tip resting against his lips as she sighed in satiated contentment. When she finally moved and sat up and ran her hands through her flaxen hair, she was once again that combination of pure loveliness and simmering sensuality. "What are you thinking?" she asked, noting his eyes studying her.

"That I didn't expect this of you," he said.

"Nor I," she smiled. "I've never seen myself this way."

"The moment, the place," Fargo shrugged.

"That's maybe part of it. The rest is you," Alison said. "Your own kind of magic." She leaned forward and pressed herself against him. "Promise me you'll work it again," she said.

"Definitely, but someplace where a Cheyenne scout might not be so apt to drop in on us," Fargo said. "Dress. We've got to move on."

She nodded and pulled on her clothes as he dressed. His eyes swept the ridges as they rode from the little lake. "Why had you come to see me?" she asked. "You said we'd talk about it later."

"I wanted you to tell Lieutenant Elliot to meet me, alone, not anyone else but him," Fargo said.

"That's out now," Alison said.

"No," Fargo said. "We'll just find another way for you to do it." He put the pinto into a canter and Alison followed as he continued upward and finally reached the ravine. Willie stepped forward, his glance taking in Alison.

"Another one?" he asked.

"Not exactly." Fargo laughed as Rita led the other girls from the wagons.

"Ladies, this is Alison Carter. She's General Carter's daughter," he introduced and turned to Alison. "These are the girls intended to satisfy Night Claw."

Alison let her eyes travel over the young women who stared at her. "I can't apologize for my father and I won't," she said. "The fact that I'm here with Fargo ought to tell you where I stand."

"That's good enough for us, honey," Rita said.

"You been practicing, I hope," Fargo said to the girls and flicked a glance at Willie. "How are they doing?" he asked.

"Hell of a lot better than I expected," Willie said with a touch of pride.

"You've one more day," Fargo said. "I'm going to try and put the last piece in place. I just stopped by to make sure that the Cheyenne hadn't stumbled onto you."

"Not yet, but I don't like stretching my luck," Willie said.

Fargo swept the young women with another quick glance. "When I come back I'll lay it all out for you," he said and motioned for Alison to follow him as he rode from the ravine.

"What now?" she asked.

"We'll find Lieutenant Elliot. That shouldn't be hard. You can be sure the general has him scouring the low hills looking for us as well as the girls this time," Fargo said and proof of his words came quickly as he spotted the platoon with the lieutenant at the head of it. Once again, Elliot sent small patrols off to search in different directions and Fargo stayed in the stand of bur oak that let him watch Elliot. He waited patiently until the lieutenant halted at a stream and let his horses drink. Fargo made his way forward, still staying in the trees and coming to a halt where the tree cover ended. Lieutenant Elliot's sincere young face was perhaps fifty yards from him, Fargo estimated, and he whispered to Alison, instructions delivered calmly yet wrapped in the tension he couldn't avoid. He was gambling on the better aspects of human nature, something he seldom did.

Alison listened intently and made no reply as she moved her horse out of the trees and approached the lieutenant at a walk. Elliot's eyes widened in surprise as he saw her and he swung onto his mount at once. "Good afternoon, Lieutenant," Alison said politely and calmly.

"Miss Carter, I have to place you under arrest," Elliot said uncomfortably. "The general's orders."

"I'm sure of that and I expected no less," Alison said. "But I've something to say to you. Right now, a .44, sixteen-shot Henry using rimfire metallic cartridges is pointed at your head. Fargo said to tell you he'd hate to have to fire it and he won't if you do exactly as I say."

Elliot's young face grew pale and he swallowed hard. "What would that be, Miss Carter?" he asked.

"He wants you to meet him alone, on the little ridge up there," she said, gesturing with one hand. "I'll stay here with your men. If anything happens to you they can take me in."

"Sounds fair enough," Elliot said, swallowing again and turned his mount toward the high ridge a few hundred yards away. He rode his horse at a walk and Fargo lowered the rifle but laid it across the saddle as the lieutenant reached the maple-covered ridge.

"Sorry the invitation had to be on these terms," Fargo said.

"General Carter issued orders to shoot you on sight," the lieutenant said.

"The general's full of strange orders. That's why I asked you up here, Lieutenant. You see, I think you know you're working for a maniac," Fargo said. "And you're smart enough to have figured out what he's doing with the saloon girls."

"He's still my superior, Fargo. He may be a maniac but he's a maniac with power," Elliot said.

"I know that and I'll be taking care of the general in my own way. But I need your help in taking care of Night Claw, first."

"How?" Elliot asked.

"I'm going to hand that Cheyenne madman a big surprise and with your help, finish him off," Fargo said. "But you have to be out patrolling again tomorrow. Tell the general you saw some signs and you're sure you're going to find the girls tomorrow. You know what he'll do, don't you?"

"He'll tell me to escort them as usual," Elliot said, his lips thinning.

"Which means desert them when the Cheyenne attack," Fargo said and Elliot looked unhappy.

"But you want me to stay and fight," Elliot said. "That'd mean disobeying an order. He'd have me court-martialed for that."

"I know and I don't want to put you in that position. You run just as you've been ordered to do. You'll hear the surprise I've in store for the Cheyenne and this time you'll stop running and come back and attack. Night Claw won't be expecting that and you won't have disobeyed orders."

Elliot's eyes brightened, a new animation flooding his face. "That's right. I'll have taken a new action in a new situation. The manual calls that initiative in the field," he said.

"You've got it," Fargo agreed. "Will you do it?"

"Yes, dammit," the lieutenant said. "I've been eaten up inside at the way we've been ordered to desert those poor girls. But lieutenants don't disagree with generals. This is different, now."

"I'll meet you at noon along the east edge of the high plain," Fargo said, as he put the rifle into its saddle holster. "You're doing the right thing, Lieutenant," he said gently. Elliot shrugged and looked hopefully uncertain as he rode away. Fargo followed him part of the distance, then halted in the trees where he could see the waiting platoon of troopers and Alison. Following his orders, Alison sent her horse bolting the minute she saw the lieutenant come into sight and she was gone before he reached the platoon. Fargo met her as she moved through the oaks and she slowed as he came alongside her. "It's done. He's going to cooperate," Fargo told her.

"You seem a little surprised. He's a decent young man," Alison said.

"I'm always surprised when I see the good side of human nature break out," Fargo said.

"Such cynicism," Alison said. "You've been badly hurt."

"Not me. I've seen too many others hurt. I've seen too many good people play it safe. I gave the lieutenant a way to salve his conscience and avoid the hard choices."

"And you're not sure what he'd have done if you hadn't given him that way," Alison said.

"Bull's eye, honey," Fargo said and put the Ovaro into a fast canter until they finally reached the ravine. He immediately gathered all the young women around him and explained his plan. Then he went through three dry runs until he was satisfied and the night descended.

"Why don't you bed down at the other end of the ravine?" Alison said when she caught a moment alone with him.

"Why not?" he said. "Nothing like a little privacy." She let a tiny smile touch her lips as she hurried away. After sharing a meal with Willie, he took his bedroll and walked along one side of the ravine until, not quite at the far end, he found a spot under a wide-branched cottonwood. He set out a blanket, undressed, and lay down on it. He didn't have to wait long before he spotted the lone figure moving down the ravine, flaxen hair a pale gold under the moonlight. "Over here," he called softly and she changed directions and reached him in moments. She wore a red robe with fake ostrich-feather fringes, he noted, and she caught his smile.

"Tillie lent it to me," she said.

"You don't look right in it," he said.

"I'll take that as a compliment," she said as she lowered herself to her knees and pushed the robe off. She was naked underneath it. Her eyes moved over his muscled symmetry and saw how he immediately responded to the sight of her loveliness. "Oh, God," she said and fell across him, rubbing her body up and down his, pressing, sliding, her mouth working hungrily on his lips, first, then down along his body. "Oh, oh . . . oh, God," he heard her gasping as she curled around him, stroking, caressing, pressing her mouth to him, even as she half screamed in sheer delight. His hands reached down and cupped her breasts as she reveled in the touch and feel of his throbbing warmth, her tongue caressing, drawing him in deeper as little moaning sounds of pleasure came from her.

Suddenly she drew away, swung over him, and plunged herself down onto him as deeply as she could go while she threw her head back and screamed. Her full, satin-smooth breasts bounced as she rose and plunged, over and over, and he pulled their wonderful fullness down to his face. Alison was half crying, half screaming as her hips writhed with every plunge, wanting to fill every inch of her deliquescent tunnel with him. He heard his own sounds of pleasure and then suddenly her breath seemed to vanish and she came down hard against him, pubic mound slamming into him. Her body stiffened and the whispered sounds fell from her open mouth. "Now, yes, now, now . . . ah, ah . . . yes . . . oh, God, oh, God," she breathed and then she was kneeling over him, trembling with the final spasms of ecstasy as he let himself join her.

Her body went limp, finally, atop his, but she stayed kneeling, holding him inside her, and her tongue licked the side of his neck, moved upward, finding his mouth, and she held there, wanting the contact of wetness to be complete. He held her gently and finally she fell away from him, onto her side and he cupped her still-trembling breasts. "Oh, God, oh my God," she breathed, gray-blue eyes staring at him from beneath the blond brows.

"I'd say you were making your own magic tonight," he commented.

"I didn't know myself again," Alison said.

"Maybe you've never known yourself," he suggested.

"I thought I did," she frowned.

"Then it must have been Tillie's robe," Fargo said and saw the small, slightly Chesire cat smile edged her lips.

"Yes, that must have been it," she said, coming against him, and was alseep in minutes. He went to sleep holding her to wake when the morning sun rose. He let himself enjoy the beauty of her as she lay still, flaxen hair and peaches-and-cream skin giving her a fairy tale, unreal quality. But he smiled as he thought about how very real she had been only hours before. He rose and began to dress and she woke, drew Tillie's robe around herself, and he caught the tiny smile on her lips as she hurried back through the ravine. He waited while the Ovaro grazed on a patch of good wheatgrass before saddling the horse. Everyone was waiting when he reached the other end of the valley, the women crammed into the two wagons, Alison and Willie to one side.

"I'll drive one wagon, you take the other, Rita," he said and his eyes went to Willie. "You ride my horse, Willie. You and Alison stay in the trees. If it goes the way I want it to go I'll wave you down. Otherwise, take care of your own necks. Hang back. I may need you later."

He slid to the ground and handed the horse to Willie as he climbed onto the first wagon. He snapped the reins and began to drive from the ravine. He drove carefully down the hill country and cast a glance back at the women in the wagons. The tension was in their faces. There was fear, too, but something else, anger and determination, and he liked that. The morning sun climbed and was at the noon mark when he reached the edge of the plains and sent the wagons rolling along the flat ground. It was only some ten minutes later when he spied the line of troopers riding toward him, Elliot in the lead, but a frown crossed his brow as the lieutenant reined to a halt. His eyes moved across the squad and back to Elliot.

"That's right, half the men I had yesterday," the lieutenant said. "The general's orders after I told him I was sure I'd find the girls today. The less troops, the more the Cheyenne would be sure to attack, he said."

"Probably true enough," Fargo said. "So start escorting us." The lieutenant nodded and deployed his weakened squad around the two wagons and waved them forward. They rode slowly, staying close to the edge of the high plains. The sun had passed into midafternoon when, peering up from under the brim of his hat, Fargo caught the faint movement in the trees. Keeping his eyes on the foliage, he watched it move in two parallel lines. He spoke in a low voice that nonetheless carried to where the lieutenant rode his mount just in front of him. "Get ready to desert us, Elliot," he said and the younger man flashed him a glance of alarm. Fargo stayed hunched up atop the driver's seat of the lead wagon when the hillside suddenly erupted with the horde of near-naked horsemen and the air was instantly filled with the high-pitched shouts.

The Cheyenne came down in three groups, firing arrows as they did, and Fargo watched Elliot take his carbine, fire back, and then give his troopers the command to run. Fargo sat motionless as the lieutenant raced past him and yelled back without turning his head. "Get that damn wagon up here," he ordered and heard Rita snapping the reins on the horse. He turned and saw her bring the second wagon alongside him, leaving a dozen feet of space between the wagons. "Now," Fargo shouted as he leaped from the driver's seat and saw the women vaulting from the wagon, pausing beside it to take hold of the one side and, with a shout, pull in unison.

The wagon went over on its side and as the army carbines fell out, each one was scooped up. He heard the crash of the second wagon as it went over to form the other half of a double barricade. Carbines were scooped up as they fell from the second wagon and Fargo's quick glance showed the women crouched behind the wagons, rifles raised, and he saw the Cheyenne racing into range. "Fire," he yelled and an explosion of sound shattered the air. He saw at least ten of the attackers go down in the first hail of bullets and the Cheyenne halted, milled in a half-circle in total surprise. A second volley of shots rang out and he saw five more braves topple from their ponies. The nearest group retreated and Fargo saw another band swooping out of the hills, circle the two wagons, and try to come in from the other side. Joined by some of the first wave, they circled and came in from the other side. But another tight volley of bullets greeted them and Fargo saw three go down.

The Cheyenne drew back, hurt and taken completely by surprise, but he watched them regroup and come in again, this time circling the wagons instead of charging. Fargo drew a bead on one, a tall, thin brave on a gray pony. He fired and the Indian went down. But the women were missing more shots now as the Cheyenne increased the speed of their circle, and with a curse he saw them send their arrows in a high, short arch that brought the shafts hurtling down inside the space between the wagons. Gasped half screams made him turn and he saw three of the women on the ground with arrows protruding from them. A half-dozen of the others started to go to their aid. "No, dammit, keep firing," Fargo roared. "You can't help them."

The women halted, hesitated, and then turned to go back to their wagon barricade. Two didn't make it as another hail of arching shafts rained down on them. Fargo flung himself sideways and narrowly avoided two arrows that plunged into the ground inches from him. He spun, peered over the side of the wagon again, and fired, two shots that brought down another circling rider. But the women were becoming unnerved, firing without taking the time to aim and missing badly. Yet he had expected that. He'd never intended or thought they could fight off the Cheyenne by themselves. They had done everything he'd wanted of them in the opening moments of the battle. Now where was Elliot, Fargo swore as he ducked another arrow that slammed into the spoke of a wheel. Where the hell was Elliot?

Another arching flight of arrows descended and he saw two more young women go down, three arrows in one, two protruding from the back of the other. The Cheyenne were breaking off their circling pattern to charge forward in small sallies, pouring a volley of arrows through the space at the front of the wagons each time. Another two women fell and Fargo saw the panic taking over the others, some no longer firing as they futilely sought a place to flee or hide. "Keep firing, dammit," he yelled and knew the command was falling on women on the edge of breaking. "Over here, give me a hand with this wagon," he shouted and six of those remaining came to put their backs and shoulders alongside him as he lifted. The wagon came up. It rocked on its wheels but stayed upright as another hail of arched arrows descended. "Under the wagon," he said as he flattened himself beneath the forward axle. He saw Rita come alongside, two others following, then another four.

He kept firing the Colt but the Cheyenne were moving in fast, from all sides, sensing final victory. Where was Elliot, Fargo cursed as he realized the truth with sickening despair. Elliot wasn't bringing his troopers back. He would have been here by now. He'd had the night to think about it and had decided to protect his career. He'd decided not to risk a confrontation with his commanding officer. Selfishness over selflessness. Career over conscience. He reloaded and kept firing and heard his own voice over the gunfire and the whoops of the Cheyenne. "You spineless little bastard, Elliot," he shouted, and knew he was cursing at all those other times he had seen the weakness inside good people.

Perhaps this would be the last time he'd witness it, he realized as the Cheyenne charged again.

# 8

Another hail of arrows descended, none finding their mark, and Fargo swore again, his eyes scanning the racing riders. There wasn't much of a chance anyone would be getting away alive from the relentless attack, but to stay under the wagons was merely to wait for the inevitable. To try was always better than to just wait and die and his eyes focused on a half-dozen riderless Indian ponies that continued to circle the wagons on their own. One came around again, not more than a dozen yards away, and Fargo glanced at the women under the wagon with him. Six, he counted. He'd need to catch a pony for himself and then corral three more. It seemed impossible. The Cheyenne would make sure that it was. But he had to try.

He waited, flattened himself, and peered along the ground until he saw the pony come around again. As it neared, he pushed himself to his knees and dived from beneath the wagon, somersaulting along the ground to come up on his feet just as the Indian pony neared. He ran and grasped hold of the rope bridle and reins with one hand and a handful of mane with the other and vaulted onto the pony. He flattened himself across the animal's back as three arrows whizzed over his head. Then he swung alongside another of the riderless ponies and grabbed hold of its rope reins.

He started back toward the wagon, looking for another

pony to seize hold of as he stayed flat. Suddenly three Cheyenne turned and started toward him. They'd be at him before he reached the wagon, he saw, and he raised the Colt to fire and the three Indians suddenly whirled and raced away. He lifted his head and saw the rest of the Cheyenne galloping toward the hillside of tree cover. He pulled the pony to a halt. His eyes moved along the flat plain and saw the double line of troopers charging up at a gallop. "Too late, goddamn you, Elliot. Too late," he flung into the wind and felt the frown dig into his brow. The lieutenant wasn't leading the platoon. The spare, trim form of General Carter rose in the forefront and Fargo found Elliot in the center of the troops.

Carter drew to a halt, his eyes malevolently staring at Fargo for a moment, then surveying the carnage that littered the ground. "Your plans didn't quite work out, did they, Fargo," the general sneered. "You see, I followed the lieutenant with my own squad when he left the compound this morning. I suspected something odd in his sudden discovery of the girls. I was watching from the trees when he left you and rode off. When he turned to go back to you I moved in."

"And stopped him," Fargo said. "You left us all to be killed."

"My plan hasn't changed," Carter said, glancing at the slain bodies of the women on the ground. "This will satisfy Night Claw for two to three weeks, enough time for me to round up more girls."

"You son of a bitch. You goddamn, twisted-up maniac," Fargo bit out.

"You're under arrest, Fargo. So is Lieutenant Elliot, by the way," Carter said.

"Why? He obeyed your goddamn orders. He left us," Fargo said.

"But it was obvious he intended to return and save you.

He was collaborating with you. Besides, he had orders to shoot you on sight and he didn't do that. I'm going to have you both shot, him for failing to obey orders and you for interfering in army business," Carter said and motioned to a corporal nearby. "Take charge of this man," he ordered. Fargo's eyes went to the lieutenant and Elliot half shrugged as he read the apology in them.

The corporal was moving toward Fargo with two troopers when the shots rang out, three of them from the tree cover. The shots blew the hats off the corporal and the two troopers who ducked, one falling from his mount. Fargo whirled the Indian pony and raced away, flattened over the animal's back as a half-dozen shots followed. Using his knees in Indian fashion, he zigzagged the pony as more shots went wild. He sat up on the mount only when he vanished into the trees. He slowed and glancing back he saw that the general hadn't sent men in chase. He brought the pony to a halt and watched Carter turn his troopers and ride back across the plain, taking the wagon with the five reamining young women.

Fargo moved the pony up the hillside through the trees and his hand yanked the Colt from its holster when he heard the sound of horses brushing back branches. He had the gun up and aimed as Willie appeared, Alison close behind him, and Fargo heard the sigh of relief escape his lips. "Thanks, Willie. That was good shooting. I owe," he said.

"Didn't want to shoot any soldier boys," Willie said.

"It was horrible, standing there watching, helpless," Alison put in.

"It was pretty horrible being in the middle of it," Fargo said as he slid from the pony, who scampered away at once. Alison moved back in the saddle as Fargo swung onto the Ovaro and rode through the trees alongside Willie.

"He'll have patrols out looking for you every day now," Willie said.

"Why didn't he send a squad chasing you just now?" Alison asked.

"There's not a lot of day left and he didn't want to chance running into a Cheyenne ambush," Fargo said. "But those weren't his real reasons. He wants to get back, go through the paperwork, and have the lieutenant shot. He wants to be sure nobody hears Elliot's side of the story. He can't afford that."

"Oh, God, how terrible," Alison murmured. "What about the other men? They must suspect just as the lieutenant did."

"They saw what's happened to Elliot. They're not going to talk, not now, not anytime so long as your father's in command," Fargo said and glanced behind him to look into Alison's eyes. "You know what I'm saying, don't you?" he said.

She nodded and looked away. "He has to be stopped," she said quietly.

"Only he holds all the cards now," Willie observed.

"First things first. I'm going to get Elliot out of there before he's put before a firing squad. I owe it to him. I asked him to help and now he's going to die for it," Fargo said. "I can't let that happen."

"How are you going to stop it, old friend?" Willie asked. "He'll have the lieutenant under heavy guard. He'll figure you might try something."

"Then I'll have to do something about that," Fargo said and Willie frowned at him as they neared the ravine.

"I think this time it is too much even for you, Fargo," Willie said.

"Maybe. I'm going to think hard on it," he said and slid from the Ovaro as they reached Willie's house and the dusk began to turn to night. Alison swung to the ground, her face grave.

"Can I help?" she asked.

"No. I want to be alone. You're a lovely distraction and I don't want distractions," he said and she nodded in understanding. He took the time to eat with her and Willie, stewed jackrabbit, and then took his bedroll deeper into the ravine and stretched out on it. He knew he had to force himself not to think about how badly everything had gone and how Wendell Carter ended up getting his way. Savagery had carried the day, the kind that came pure and undisguised and the kind that hid behind a mask of civilized behavior.

He swore silently and pushed aside his thoughts. He could concentrate on only one thing and he had to clear his mind for that. He lay awake, staring into the dark velvet that was the sky, letting thoughts come to him on their own, willing his mind to find a way. The night grew deep and he lay awake, rejecting thoughts, discarding, examining, refusing, sometimes almost in a kind of trance. The moon was sliding down the distant sky to the horizon when he sat up, his eyes snapping open. He turned thoughts again in his mind before he lay back, and this time he slept until the morning sun woke him.

Willie had coffee on and Alison, in a dark-blue shirt and black skirt, poured a mug for him as he arrived. He took it and gratefully sipped the strong, hot brew. "You come up with something," Willie said. "It's in your eyes."

"The only thing that might work. It was something you said that made it come together, Willie," Fargo answered. "You said this time it was too much, even for me." Willie nodded and Fargo's smile was grim. "You were right. I'll never get to Elliot alone. I'll need help. I'll need a diversion, a big diversion. There's only one way I can get that. I need Night Claw to attack the compound."

"You get a bullet in your head, Fargo?" Willie frowned. "What makes you think Night Claw attack compound for you?"

"Not for me. For his honor as a great chief. He's going to learn that the bluecoat chief has been laughing at him, making a fool out of him and talking about it. That'll be a direct blow at all he stands for in the eyes of his people. You know that, WIllie."

"That's true." Willie nodded. "A great chief can take defeat but not dishonor. He will be very angry."

"Angry enough to avenge his honor in the only way he can, by killing the man who brought dishonor to him," Fargo said.

Willie nodded again. "Only who's going to tell him?"

"We are," Fargo said and disbelief flooded the small man's leathery face. "I'll talk. You translate. You speak Algonkian a lot better than I do."

"And then we be dead," Willie said.

"No, I've too much unfinished business for that," Fargo said.

"You crazy, Fargo," Willie muttered.

Alison cut in, concern laced with reproach in her voice. "Do you hear what you're saying, Fargo? You're setting up a surprise attack by Night Claw. What about all the troopers who'll be killed by that?"

"I don't want that to happen. The general will be warned about the attack," Fargo said.

"How?" Alison questioned.

"You'll ride down and tell him," he said and saw the surprise swirl through Alison's face.

"What if he doesn't believe me? He's so suspicious about anything I say now," Alison said.

"I'll have done my part," Fargo said grimly. "I can't do more."

"I guess not," Alison said gravely. "You know that whether he believes me or not he'll keep me prisoner. You'll have more than the lieutenant to rescue."

"It'll be two for the price of one," Fargo said.

"There's a kind of poetic justice to it," Alison said, thinking aloud. "You're arranging a final showdown between two men who are each mad in their own way."

"There'll only be justice in it if I can stop Elliot from facing a firing squad," Fargo said. "Willie and I will be leaving soon for Night Claw's camp. You stay in this ravine till we get back."

"Don't worry. I'm not going anywhere," Alison said and Fargo turned from her and brought the Ovaro around. Using his lariat, he fashioned a bridle in the Indian fashion and did the same for Willie's horse.

"No saddles, either," he told Willie when he was finished. "Night Claw might have sentries out now, just in case the army follows tracks of his braves. I want to get close to his camp with the horses." Willie nodded in understanding and when he was ready to leave, Fargo found Alison's arms around him.

"God, be careful," she murmured as her lips pressed his.

"Count on it," he said. He held her a moment longer as a reminder of one more piece of unfinished business and then he swung onto the warm, bare back of the Ovaro and rode from the ravine with Willie. He didn't hurry, moving carefully along the high country and watching the sun slowly arc its way toward the end of the day.

"You know how many things can go wrong in this crazy business?" Willie asked. "I been counting to myself."

"Fill me in," Fargo said.

"One, we never leave Cheyenne camp alive. Two, general won't believe his daughter and Night Claw wipes out compound before you have chance to save lieutenant. Three, you get killed trying to get into compound in middle of battle. Four, you free lieutenant and you both get shot by soldiers or Cheyenne. Five, crazy general shoots lieutenant tonight and everything is for nothing. General still wins. Six, you go to compound and wait for Night Claw to attack and you can't do a damn thing without it but there is no attack because Night Claw is afraid you come to draw him into trap." Willie paused and cast a jaundiced glance at Fargo. "That enough?" he grunted.

"More than enough," Fargo said. "But you forget one thing. It all goes the way I planned it."

"Like with the women and the wagons?" Willie returned and Fargo felt his mouth grow thin.

"You want to turn back? I'll go it alone. No hard feelings, old friend," he said.

"Didn't say that," Willie grunted.

"Why are you staying?" Fargo questioned.

"Night Claw mean big trouble for everybody if he wins. Night Claw is a crazy chief. You have crazy general, we have crazy chief," Willie said.

"Fair enough," Fargo said as the dusk came to settle over the land. The night followed and grew deep before they reached the Cheyenne camp and Fargo threaded his way through the forest of oak, the smell of the Indian camp curling into his nostrils. His eyes searched the forest but he saw no sentries. Night Claw was as big an egotist as the general. Fargo moved closer on the horses with no smell of saddle leather and no sound of rein chains to jeopardize their approach. The camp was suddenly in full view as he halted, mostly asleep with only a few figures still stirring, and he pointed to the large teepee at the far end. He moved the horses closer to the teepee, Willie alongside him, and halted again, this time sliding to the ground. Fargo used sign language to speak to Willie and made the sign for waiting and Willie dropped to one knee.

His eyes sweeping the camp, Fargo watched the few still-awake figures settle down, two braves entering a teepee, another three stretching out on the ground. Taking no chances, he allowed another half hour and then began to creep to the rear of the large teepee, flattening himself on the ground as he reached the buckskin tent. The Cheyenne were one of the tribes that preferred the wide-based teepee and the long bottom edge allowed more flexibility than the narrower teepee. His cheek pressed against the ground, he edged the bottom of the teepee upward enough to peer inside. A flickering light was the first thing he saw, a circle of tallow burning inside a hollowed piece of rock. His eyes moved around the interior of the teepee and found the Cheyenne chief asleep on a mat made of dried strap fern.

He was naked except for two items, a small strip of hide across his groin and the necklace of turkey claws. Fargo drew the thin-bladed throwing knife from his calf holster and slid under the edge of the tent and held it open for Willie to wriggle his smaller body inside. Rising to the tips of his toes, Fargo crossed the interior of the teepee and pressed the tip of the blade against the Cheyenne chief's neck. Night Claw woke instantly and sat up and Fargo kept the tip of the knife against his throat as the Indian pushed to his feet.

"This man will kill you if you do the wrong thing," Willie told the chief in Algonkian.

Fargo moved to one side so Night Claw could see the old Remington .44 double-action pistol in Willie's hand. The Cheyenne's eyes burned with black fire as he stared at Fargo and Willie translated the words he growled.

"He says you are a dead man. Me, too," Willie said. "He wants to know why you have been such a fool to come here?"

"How many fools have come into your camp?" Fargo asked as Willie translated. Night Claw stared back but he had taken in the answer.

"I came to see the chief who has been made a fool by the bluecoat chief," Fargo said. "None of the women the bluecoat chief has given you were settler's women. They were nothing thrown at you so he could laugh at you and tell everyone you are no chief, just a stupid fool who calls himself a chief."

Fargo saw the hatred blazing in the pits of the black eyes. "Why have you come here to tell me this?" the Cheyenne asked.

"The bluecoat chief told me to come. He dares you to meet him in battle on the high plain," Fargo said and waited for Willie to translate. "He tells everyone that Night Claw is not only a fool but a coward, afraid to fight his soldiers." The Cheyenne chief's jaw throbbed with rage. "The bluecoat chief wants an answer. What will I tell him?" Fargo pressed.

"You will not leave here alive to tell him anything," Night Claw rasped.

Fargo transferred the knife to his left hand and drew the Colt from its holster and held it by the barrel. The Cheyenne's eyes were slits of hate as he realized what Fargo planned to do. "I'll leave here alive and tell him the great Night Claw is too afraid to answer," Fargo said.

"Tell him I will kill him and all his soldiers," the chief said. "And I will kill you, too. Night Claw will not forget this."

"Me neither," Fargo said and Willie didn't bother to translate as the butt of the Colt crashed down on the Indian's temple. Night Claw's powerful form crumpled to the ground and Fargo returned the knife to its calf holster and was at the edge of the teepee in three long-legged strides. He lay down on his stomach, picked up the edge of the tent, and listened, then slid himself outside. Willie followed, and rising to a crouch, Fargo moved toward the trees where they had left the horses. He climbed onto the pinto and held the horse to a walk as he rode away from the Cheyenne camp. He waited till they were far enough from the Cheyenne camp before he spoke to Willie. "So far so good," he said. "Night Claw's burning up with rage."

"What if he goes to meet the general on the high plain?" Willie asked.

"He won't. He won't risk the rest of his braves in an open field battle with the army. He'll do what he thinks Carter won't expect, attack the compound. He knows he'll have the advantage of surprise and terrain," Fargo said and put the pinto into a trot downhill. "It's been put into motion, Willie. Now I have to be ready to do the right thing at the right time at the right place."

"Only five things to go wrong now," Willie grunted and Fargo refused to answer though he knew how very right the little man was.

# 9

They reached the ravine soon after morning dawned and Alison was clinging to him in moments. "You're on next," he said to her as she pulled her lips from his.

"I'm ready," she said and he turned to Willie Moccasin as she saddled her horse.

"Thanks for everything, old friend," Fargo said.

"I'm coming," Willie said.

"No reason for that. I've got to go in alone. It's the only way it has a chance to work," Fargo said.

"I'll watch from the hills. Nobody see me. I'm not staying here wondering what happened. If Night Claw wins I'm leaving ravine real fast," Willie said and Fargo nodded. Willie's point was all too understandable.

"Let's go," Fargo said as Alison appeared on her horse. They rode downhill mostly in silence until they began to draw closer to the compound. "Here's where you leave us," Fargo said to Alison.

"You think the Cheyenne will attack tonight?" she asked.

"Not during the night. Like most tribes, the Cheyenne don't much like night fighting. They'll attack at dawn," Fargo said.

"Father will ask why you didn't bring him the warning yourself instead of sending me," Alison said.

"Tell him I don't like being shot on sight. He ought to buy that," Fargo said and Alison leaned from her mount to kiss him, a brief touch of soft lips and then she was moving away, downhill as Fargo watched with Willie a few paces behind. When she vanished from sight, Fargo swung to the ground. "We'll give her plenty of time to get there. Besides, I'm not going to show till after dark." Willie nodded but stayed in the saddle and when the sun began to slide from view over the far hills, Fargo climbed back onto the Ovaro and started downhill.

Night descended quickly as he carefully drew closer to the compound area, but still staying in the trees. He slowed as he heard Willie stop. "I go find my own place from here," Willie said. "Good luck." Fargo smiled and clasped hands with the little man who moved his horse east into the trees. Fargo continued down the slope. As he halted in the trees he saw by the moon that it was almost midnight. The trees were almost at a level with the stockade and the army tents which lay in a double row outside its walls. His eyes swept the tents and his lips drew back in a grimace. He saw but two troopers on sentry duty, one at each end of the tents.

Carter hadn't believed Alison's warning. Fargo was not surprised but he'd let himself hope and he swore softly at the general's blindness. He edged closer to the stockade before he dismounted and tethered the pinto to a low branch out of sight in the tree cover. Going forward on foot, his lariat in one hand, he dropped to one knee where the treeline ended and the stockade rose up some twenty yards away. His eyes went to the dark, dense blackness that was the tree-covered hills, rising up less than a hundred yards from the double row of tents. The Cheyenne were perhaps already making their way down inside the thick foliage. They would be neither heard nor seen, silent and stealthy as the forest serpents. Until they were ready to explode into action. He had to be ready then, positioned and waiting for the diversion he needed.

He crept sideways along the edge of the treeline until he faced the rear of the stockade wall. The Cheyenne would swoop down on the tents, first, he was certain. Since they would be on the flat ground they would be able to pour arrows into the troops that came through the stockade gate. A proper commander would keep his remaining troops behind the stockade walls, not charging out to rescue men largely beyond saving. But Wendell Carter would think nothing of sacrificing more men to satisfy his own image of himself and Fargo felt the bitterness swirl inside him. He measured the height of the pointed stockade posts with his eyes as the moon began to dip beyond the hills. His hands were damp with perspiration and he wiped them dry as the first faint streaks of pink began to touch the sky.

Clutching the lariat, feeling the tenseness of his body, he watched the sky begin to grow light. The trees were more than a dense mass of blackness now as they took shape and suddenly he saw the movement along the base of the hill. He half rose from his knees, waiting for the racing ponies to break into sight, but the frown dug into his brow as he heard the hissing sound and saw the arrows, some two dozen of them and each tipped by a blazing ball of fire. They sprang from the trees as if by themselves and hurtled into the wooden walls of the stockade, where flames instantly began to leap upward along the dry wood fence. The second sound was an even greater surprise, the sharp staccato of rifle fire, and then he saw the ponies breaking into view, racing toward the tents while their riders poured rifle fire into the triangles of canvas. Night Claw had been holding back. Somewhere, somehow, he had amassed enough rifles for two dozen of his warriors.

As half-dressed, half-awake troopers fell from their tents they were mowed down in the hail of rifle fire while others never left the tents alive. Shouts and the sounds of men racing to arms came from inside the stockade, which was now burning in over a dozen places. Fargo raced toward the rear wall where flames leaped up the wooden stockade posts in at least three places. He flung the lariat, catching the loop around the pointed top of one of the posts, and yanked it tight and began to pull himself up on the rope. A burst of wind sent a tongue of flame at him and kicking hard against the wood with both feet, he swung himself away from the fiery fingers. New desperation giving him new strength, he pulled himself upward again as smoke blew across his face from the stockade fence, which was rapidly being consumed by flames.

Reaching the top, he climbed over and, clutching the lariat, he began to lower himself down the other side. He saw confusion and near chaos inside the compound below as troopers were running to the compound gate, dropping to their knees to form a battle line as they fired at the Cheyenne, who charged past the gate firing back with arrows and bullets. Fargo hit the ground and glimpsed Carter near the stockade gate, behind the fence, shouting orders in an effort to rally a defense. A section of the stockade became a tower of flames and collapsed to the ground as Fargo raced across the compound to the guardhouse, which had been left deserted. He burst into the door, the Colt in his hand, and saw Elliot behind the bars of the cell.

"Jesus, what's going on out there?" the lieutenant asked.

"All hell," Fargo bit out as he blew the lock apart on the cell door with a single shot. Elliot bolted from the cell and followed Fargo outside, where he saw the scene with horror seizing his face. "Get two rifles and meet me at the general's quarters," Fargo said and ran along the edge of the barracks as Elliot raced to the arms shed. The door to Carter's quarters hung open and Fargo raced in to the rear room to find Alison bound to a chair in wrist irons. A rush of relief as she saw him pushed the panic from her eyes.

"There's a key in the table drawer," she said and Fargo yanked the drawer open, saw the thick, short key and was opening the wrist irons when the lieutenant appeared with the rifles. Fargo took one from him and handed it to Alison.

"Damn near one wall of the stockade is down," Elliot said as Fargo brushed past him to the door of the building. He swept the scene with a single, all-encompassing glance. Those troopers still alive were firing from small pockets of defense they had formed along the barracks wall. Cheyenne raced in and out of the compound through the section where the wall had fallen as well as through the gate. They used the cover of the smoke to dart forward, fire their arrows, and race away. The smoke made accurate fire difficult for both sides, but the Cheyenne were hurtling arrows in clusters, depending on some finding a target, their tactics dismissing the need for marksmanship.

Fargo swept the scene again and found Carter crouched near the stable with a half-dozen troopers, firing a carbine at Cheyenne who came within range. Without much accuracy, Fargo noted as he saw the man miss two shots. The ground was strewn with bodies, some Cheyenne, but most half-clothed in uniforms. But the initial force of the attack had diminished, Fargo saw. The attackers were racing around the burning stockade more in the jubilation of victory, now. They'd slay the few defenders still left but they could do so without losing more warriors in direct attacks. They'd finish the job in their own way and in their own time. Fargo swore inwardly as he realized there was only one way to prevent that. They'd withdraw if their chief was dead.

He turned to the lieutenant. "I'm putting Alison in your hands, Elliot," he said. "Stay here as long as you can. It's the safest place for now."

"Yes, sir," the young man said gravely. "I'll make a break for it only if I see a chance."

"That'll be your call, Lieutenant," Fargo said.

"Thanks for coming for me, Fargo," Elliot said. "I'm sure you didn't expect to run into this."

"Guess again," Fargo said and Elliot frowned.

"What are you going to do?" Alison asked Fargo, her hand on his arm.

"Try to find us a last chance," he said and stepped outside. He glanced across to the stable and enjoyed seeing the combination of surprise and rage on Carter's face as the man saw him. Dropping into a crouch, Fargo started across the compound through a swirl of smoke toward the section of the wall that had toppled to the ground. He had almost reached it when, materializing out of a roll of blue-gray smoke, the Indian pony appeared directly in front of him. Fargo drew the Colt in one lightninglike motion as the Cheyenne raised his bow to fire his arrow at point-blank range. But the arrow never left the bow as Fargo's shot slammed into the red man's midsection and he toppled forward. He clung to his pony for a moment and then fell to the ground.

Fargo raced around the horse and across the smoldering pieces of the stockade wall. Outside, he halted, dropped to one knee, and searched the scene. His eyes came to rest on the pony standing alone at the edge of the trees, the near-naked muscled form sitting quietly atop it. Night Claw motioned with his hands, small, quick gestures first to one group of his warriors, then another. He was fully in command of the situation, still directing his warriors, commanding the scene, and Fargo leaped to his feet and let out a thunderous roar. The Cheyenne chief's head swiveled, his black eyes narrowing at once as he found Fargo. Staying in a crouch, Fargo ran across the clear space toward the trees where he had left the Ovaro. With a quick glance behind, he saw Night Claw spur his pony forward to come after him and Fargo straightened from the crouch, dug his heels into the ground, and streaked for the trees. He plunged into the foliage, found the Ovaro, and flung himself into the saddle as he loosened the tether.

He spun the horse and started up the hill as he heard Night Claw's pony crashing into the trees just behind him. The Ovaro's power let it climb steadily but Fargo heard the chief's pony gaining ground, lighter and quicker, able to dodge through the thickly forested terrain. Spying an old and largely overgrown deer trail, Fargo sent the pinto along its straight path while he heard Night Claw stay in the thick tree cover. The Indian heard him, also, and knew where he was, Fargo realized. This was not a game of stealth, not yet. It was a contest of positioning, seizing opportunity, for the moment. But before it ended, it would be a battle of every skill he could summon, he realized. The deer trail ended in a sudden downhill stretch and Fargo glimpsed the small circle of partly cleared land at the bottom. He sent the Ovaro downward, crossed the small area, and plunged into the trees surrounding it, where he pulled to a halt.

He leaped from the horse, the Colt in hand, and dropped to one knee and almost smiled as the sound of Night Claw's pony abruptly ended. The Indian had realized his quarry had stopped running and Fargo's eyes swept the edges of the small, clear area. He knew that Night Claw was on foot now, also. But to come at him the Cheyenne would have to cross the clear space or make his way around the edges. Either way, he'd pick up the Indian's approach, Fargo was certain, and he remained motionless, hardly breathing, his eyes sweeping back and forth along the edges of the clearing. But he caught no movement in the trees, no glimpse of a shadowed shape. Perhaps Night Claw had decided to also play the waiting game, Fargo pondered. He was still musing at the thought when the sudden, soft swish of air caught at him.

He whirled just in time to see the tomahawk hurtling at him from out of the tree branches. He tried to pull away but the short-handled ax struck him in the right shoulder. It was not a direct blow that imbedded the tomahawk into his shoulder, but a glancing blow that sent the ax skittering off to the side. Fargo felt the pain shoot through his entire arm and he knew the Colt had dropped from his grip as he looked upward and saw the Cheyenne chief in the tree. Fargo swore at himself. Night Claw had climbed from tree to tree with the silence of a lynx and Fargo saw the Indian leaping down from the tree.

Fargo groaned in pain as he tried to use his right arm and found it entirely numb. The Cheyenne hit the ground in front of him, the wild turkey claw necklace bouncing as he landed and he drew a jagged-edged skinning knife from his loincloth thong. Fargo moved in a circle and edged toward the cleared patch of ground, aware that he could never move fast enough in the thicket of trees. Night Claw, his mouth twisted into a grin of anticipation, advanced toward him and Fargo feinted to the left with his body and saw the quickness of the Indian as Night Claw slashed out with the knife.

The Cheyenne came forward again and Fargo retreated, glancing to his left to see the cleared area but a half-dozen feet away, and he turned and ran, bursting through the trees. He was facing Night Claw, his feet planted firmly in the grass of the clearing, as the Indian came out of the trees. Night Claw feinted to his right, then slashed to his left, and Fargo spun away. He tried to bring his right arm up but there was only the unresponding numbness and Fargo flung himself sideways to barely avoid another slash of the knife. Night Claw was after him at once, swiping with a tremendous upward blow that tore through the side of Fargo's shirt. As Fargo leaped away again, he hit the ground and gasped at the pain in his numbed arm as he rolled and came up on his feet. Reaching down with his left hand, he drew the thin-bladed throwing knife from its calf holster and began to circle his foe. He tried a feinting swipe and cursed at how awkward it felt using his left arm.

He tried another two swipes, which Night Claw avoided with disdainful ease, stepping forward and thrusting with his own blade. Fargo had to pull his abdomen in as he flung himself backward to avoid the point of the Indian's knife. He let himself seem to stumble sideways and Night Claw leaped in to take advantage of the moment. But Fargo dropped to his hands and knees and as the Indian's blow passed over him, Night Claw fell across his back. Fargo came up, sending the Cheyenne sprawling on the other side of him, and leaped forward with a slashing blow of the double-edged blade. The Cheyenne managed to twist away, but not before a gash opened across his shoulder blade.

Regaining his feet as he felt the blood running down his back, Night Claw let out a roar of rage and leaped forward, slicing viciously with the skinning knife, one blow after the other, right and left and right again, and Fargo could only pull away, duck, twist, and fall backward. Had the knife been in his right hand he would have struck back and tried to slip a thrust in between the Cheyenne chief's slashing blows. He started to try and knew at once it would be a fatal mistake. He hadn't the split-second muscle coordination and speed with his left hand to make a dangerous counterstrike work and he drew back. He stepped left and tried to move his right arm again and found that though the numbness was still there he could feel a tingling as nerves and muscles strained to regain their usefulness.

Could he hold out long enough, he wondered with grim desperation as Night Claw came in again. It would be only a matter of time before he slowed enough to let one of the Cheyenne's blows land and he saw Night Claw stalking him, eyes pieces of black coal. The Cheyenne was also aware that all he had to do was keep slicing and slashing and his foe would give him the chance to strike the fatal blow. Fargo backtracked to the edge of the trees and saw he was near the spot where the tomahawk had struck to send the Colt from his hand. If he could find the gun the odds would suddenly change and he turned and dived into the trees, pushing aside branches as his eyes searched the overgrown forest floor.

He heard Night Claw charging into the trees after him, the Indian suddenly realizing what he was trying to find. Fargo swore as he kicked at leaves and rocks but the Colt remained hidden under the carpet of leaves and forest brush. Then he saw a length of stout oak branch on the ground, perhaps two feet long and a good six inches in diameter. He took hold of it, tried using both hands, and found he could lift his right arm a fraction. Spinning, he raced out of the trees and back into the clearing with the branch, where he halted less than a foot from the trees. He thrust the thin throwing knife into his belt and dropped to one knee, holding the branch in front of him in ramrod fashion. Night Claw charged out of the treeline and Fargo sprung forward, the thick length of branch held out in front of him. He clasped it firmly with his left arm, and with a roar he smashed it into the Indian's chest.

Night Claw shouted in pain as the necklace of wild turkey claws were driven through his chest and he halted, stumbling backward, and still shouting in pain, tore the claw necklace out of his chest, leaving a dozen streaks of blood coursing down his torso. It all took seconds but seconds were all Fargo needed to pull the throwing knife from his belt and fling it. The thin, double-edged blade hurtled the short distance, not with the force it would have had had he thrown it with his right hand, but enough to imbed itself into the Cheyenne's solar plexus, just above the half-circle of blood rivulets that ran down his torso.

But as he watched with surprise and horror, Night Claw grasped the throwing knife by its handle and tore it out of himself with an astounding display of strength and fury. Blood spraying into the air, he held a knife in each hand and flung himself forward, his arms upraised to bring both weapons down on his target. Fargo crouched, his left arm upraised to seize one of the Indian's wrists. He grimaced as he tried to raise his right arm, and he managed to get it half up as the numbness still clung. But half up was not good enough, he knew, nor was grabbing hold of one of the Indian's wrists. He flung himself backward onto the ground as Night Claw rose up before him and hit hard. Fargo felt the shock go through his right arm but he kicked out with both his powerful legs. His feet caught the Indian in the groin and the man, in pain and off balance, dropped to his knees and missed hitting his target with both knives.

Fargo scuttled backward, crab fashion, and pushed to his feet, raising his right arm, and it responded and he felt the strength surging through it. Somehow, hitting the ground had shocked the numbness away and he wasn't about to wonder how or why. Night Claw regained his feet, still holding both knives as he came forward. But his mouth was hanging open, Fargo saw, and blood was pouring from his chest, mostly from the hole in his solar plexus. Yet he came on, strong legs still carrying him, but now Fargo feinted, a quick shoulder movement, and Night Claw swiped with one knife, then the other. Fargo moved lightly, coaxing Night Claw into another energy-consuming series of slashes, and he saw the Cheyenne's breathing coming hard now. Fargo halted, half crouched, and Night Claw gathered himself and charged, both knives upraised to strike.

This time, Fargo measured split-seconds, as he ducked under the two swiping slashes. He stuck out one foot as he flung himself sideways. Night Claw struck his foot, tripped, and went facedown on the ground. He was starting to pull himself up, moving with heavy slowness now, when Fargo landed on the small of his back with both feet, putting all his strength and weight behind the leap. The blow flattened Night Claw into the ground and Fargo jumped back, half crouched, and started to leap onto the Indian again but Night Claw didn't move. Fargo halted, every muscle tensed, watching the prostrate form of the Cheyenne, but it lay still. He took a careful step closer, well aware that the Cheyenne knew how to play possum. He nudged the man with the tip of his foot and there was no movement. Reaching down, he pulled on the Indian's upper arm and turned him over. Both knives were driven deeply into Night Claw's chest, where he had come down hard on them when Fargo had landed on his back.

It was over and Fargo allowed himself a long breath as he reached down and pulled the throwing knife from the Cheyenne. He had just finished wiping it clean on the grass and returned it to its calf holster when the voice drifted across the small clearing to him. "I'm glad it's you, not that I really cared much either way," the voice said and Fargo turned to see Wendell Carter on his horse, the carbine held steady, a sneering smile touching his lips. "One more surprise, Fargo, your last one," he said.

"You were watching," Fargo said. "Waiting to see him kill me."

"Yes," Carter admitted. "I really expected he would."

"Then you'd have killed him," Fargo said.

"Yes, everything wrapped up neatly," Carter said. "It'll be just as neat this way. I'll actually enjoy killing you more than I would have him."

"Naturally. You were brothers in madness," Fargo said. "How'd you get away?"

"I saw him go after you. When he left, the others fell back and waited. I saw a chance to get out and follow him. When I'm through with you I'll go back and finish the lieutenant. There'll be no one left to accuse me of anything," Carter said smugly.

"Alison will be left. She knows about all of it, so why don't you just go back with me or are you going to kill your own daughter, too?" Fargo said.

"That will depend on Alison," Carter said and Fargo stared at the man as the numbing horror of the answer crept through him.

"You mad, twisted son of a bitch," Fargo murmured. Carter shrugged and start to bring the carbine up a fraction of an inch. Fargo dived, twisted his body, hit the ground, and rolled as the first shot passed over him. He flung himself into the trees. But he had learned the futility of trying to find the Colt while being pursued and this time he struck out for where he'd left the Ovaro. He reached the horse and pulled the big Henry from its saddle case as Carter appeared through the trees. Fargo fired two fast shots and saw the blue-uniformed figure retreat at once.

Fargo followed but refused to let anger destroy caution and he ducked behind the trunk of an oak as Carter fired two shots. The man turned and was running again, Fargo heard, and he stepped from behind the tree to give chase. This time Carter didn't turn to fire again and Fargo saw him reach the edge of the trees and start to race across the clearing. "Damn," Fargo swore as he ran forward. Carter was racing to his horse and he had almost reached it when Fargo stepped into the clearing and raised the rifle.

"Drop the gun," he called out but Carter whirled, firing a scatter-shot volley as he did, and Fargo had to drop to the ground as the hail of bullets cut through the air all around him. Carter flung the empty weapon aside as Fargo rose to his feet, the Henry aimed.

"You won't shoot," Carter said, facing him defiantly.

"What the hell makes you think I won't?" Fargo threw back.

"You don't want to have to tell Alison you killed her father," Carter said and almost laughed. Fargo realized that the thought that welled up inside him was not a sudden decision. It had lain inside him, in his subconscious, only to explode in shape and form by the moment.

"You're right," Fargo said, aimed, and pulled the trigger.

"Ow, Jesus, Jesus," Carter screamed as the bullet shattered his right kneecap. He fell and clutched at his leg just below where his right kneecap had been. "Oh, Jesus," he cried out again. Fargo still had the rifle to his shoulder and his finger tightened on the trigger again. Wendell Carter's scream of excruciating pain echoed across the clearing as his left kneecap shattered in a shower of blood and bone. "Jesus, oh, God, oh, Jesus," he screamed as he lay on the ground and pounded both fists into the soil. He managed to look up, his eyes blazing with rage and pain as he found Fargo moving closer. "You bastard. You stinking, rotten bastard," he flung out between cries of pain. "I'll never walk again."

"You'll never command a troop again, either," Fargo said as he started to walk past the man's trembling body.

"Jesus, you can't leave me. I'll bleed to death. You've got to help me," Carter cried out in sudden panic.

"I'm not leaving. You've still got things to do," Fargo said, looking down at the man. "Wait right here," he said.

"Goddamn fucking bastard," Carter roared and screamed as a bolt of pain shot through him. Fargo walked away and stepped into the trees on the other side of the clearing, where he halted, listened, and finally picked up the sound he sought. He followed it to where Night Claw's pony tore at the buds of low-branched leaves. He approached the pony slowly and the animal didn't shy and he reached out and took hold of its rawhide bridle and led it back to the clearing.

He passed Carter, who moaned on the ground, halted beside the Cheyenne chief's body, lifted the man, and draped him facedown across the pony's back. Fargo grimaced as he stepped back. The Indian had been a heavy, dead weight and the gash on his own shoulder throbbed. But he turned and stepped to where Carter's eyes held bitter rage and pain. He brought the army mount around closer, reached down, and lifted the general by his belt and the back of his uniform. "Oh, Jesus, easy . . . .oh, God, it hurts, oh, Jesus," Carter screamed.

"Screw easy," Fargo snapped as he deposited Carter in the saddle and the man screamed in pain again as rivers of blood coursed down his legs. Fargo went to the other side of the army mount, seized the general by one thigh, and swung him around in the saddle as Carter shrieked and fell forward, his arms clutching the front of the saddle, his chest against the pommel.

"Oh, God, oh, God, the pain . . . oh, the pain," he moaned.

"I'm sorry," Fargo said and Carter frowned at him.

"You're sorry?" he managed to mutter.

"Yes. I keep thinking about all those girls you sacrificed

147

to the Cheyenne and I'm sorry I can't make it worse," he said, turned away, and climbed onto the Ovaro. He gathered the reins of the general's mount and the Cheyenne rawhide halter and slowly made his way downhill. Wendell Carter's pain-filled moaning was one of the most pleasant sounds he'd heard in a long time, he remarked to himself as he rode along deer trails and finally he smelled the odor of smoke and charred wood. He came in sight of the stockade to find only one wall standing and he saw the Cheyenne warriors in a half-circle around the remains of the compound.

They rose, those on the ground, quickly climbing onto their horses as Fargo let go of the general's mount, which came to a halt. Leading the pony, Fargo advanced on the Cheyenne warriors, and one, a thin-framed man, came forward alone. Fargo offered the pony to him, and his face stone, the Indian took the rawhide halter and gestured with one hand to the bodies of other Cheyenne on the ground. Fargo nodded and with a wave of his arm, the Indian sent others forward to pick up their dead. Fargo backed the Ovaro away, returned to where Carter lay half sobbing now over his saddle, and led the horse into the compound.

Lieutenant Elliot and half a dozen troopers rushed to him and lifted Carter from the horse and carried him to his quarters. "You've a medical corpsman here?" Fargo asked.

"Yes, sir," Elliot said.

"Have him stop the blood flow best he can. You've a supply wagon, too, I'd guess," Fargo said and the lieutenant nodded. "I'll be taking the general to Miles Stanford. They've a field hospital unit there," Fargo said. As Elliot hurried after the troops carrying Carter into his quarters, Fargo swung to the ground and Alison raced into his arms and buried her flaxen hair into his chest.

"Oh, thank God you're back alive and it's over," she murmured.

"Almost," he said and she looked up at him, searching his face. "Where are those papers you wanted signed?" he asked and the smile took a moment to come before it edged her lips.

"I'll get them," she said, and hurried away.

Fargo let his gaze sweep the scene. The compound buildings were intact. The stockade could be erected again. The grimness came over him as he saw troopers collecting the bodies of their slain comrades. Lives could not be erected again, he murmured bitterly. He turned and strode into Carter's quarters, where the general lay propped up in a bed as the medical corpsman finished the thick wadding of bandages around both Carter's knees. "It's the best I can do, sir," the soldier said.

"It'll do. Leave us alone," Fargo said and the corpsman hurried out.

"You don't give orders to my men," Carter said, wincing with pain as he moved his shoulders to sit up straighter.

"Neither do you, not anymore," Fargo said and pulled open a drawer of a desk to find a box of official army stationery. He handed Carter one of the sheets and a pad to write on. "Start writing what I tell you to write," he said.

"You're not giving me orders," Carter bristled.

Fargo drew the Colt and placed it against the man's temple. "You're right. I'm giving you a last chance to stay alive. Now, you listen to me, you twisted, arrogant bastard. I'd just as soon kill you if I had my way. Alison's the only thing keeping you alive and if you strain my patience anymore even she won't be enough, you understand?"

Carter's face blanched and his tongue darted out to lick lips suddenly dry. Fargo drew the Colt back six inches. "Talk," Carter said.

"Two separate sheets. First one, you give the lieutenant a field promotion to captain and put him in command of this post." Carter began to write as Fargo looked on. His pen halted when he finished, trembling at the place for his signature. Fargo pulled the hammer back on the Colt and Carter signed. Fargo handed him another sheet of the official stationery. "Now you're going to resign your command here and resign from active duty. Your kneecaps will see to that but I want it all said formal and proper. I want to be sure I never hear of you having anything to do with active duty again."

Carter groaned as pain shot through him and he began to write again. He had just signed the letter when Alison appeared carrying the papers in her hand. "Now you'll sign these papers," Fargo said and Alison handed her father the papers.

"You've become quite a disappointment to me, Alison," Carter said as he put his signature on the papers.

"You've become a terrible shame to me," Alison said, snatching the signed papers back and turning away.

"Get your things together and tell Elliot to have the wagon ready," Fargo told her and she hurried outside. His lake-blue eyes were as cold as a January ice floe as he stared down at Carter. "I'm going to tell Miles Stanford about the Cheyenne attack but I'm not going to file a report about what you did. You know why, you stinkin' piece of shit? Because a report would have to become part of the official and public record and I don't want that. You and your twisted mind have already hurt enough innocent people. It'd be a shame for the reputation and the standards of all the good men in the United States Army if it became known that a sick bastard like you was put in command of a post." He turned and paused at the door to look back at Carter. "Say the wrong thing or do the wrong thing and I'll just shoot you and be done with it," he added and strode outside where the lieutenant was bringing the supply wagon around with two men. "Lay him inside," Fargo said and saw Alison appear carrying her things. "We'll go all the way, no stopping except to water the horses, and damn little talking," he said.

"I understand," she said and climbed into the driver's seat beside him as he took the reins of the two horses. He waited till the general lay groaning in pain in the back of the wagon. Lieutenant Elliot saluted crisply as Fargo drove from the compound. Outside, he glanced up at the low hills and saw the wiry figure atop the horse, quietly watching. He waved and Willie Moccasin raised an arm and waved back and Fargo smiled. Old friends didn't need words.

# 10

A night had passed since Wendell Carter had been brought into the base, where the doctors quickly attended to him, and now General Miles Stanford studied the big man who sat across from him. "Quite a battle from the way you tell it, Fargo," the general said. "But I guess all's well that ends well. It's a rotten shame Carter lost so many good men but the Cheyenne chief is dead."

"He is." Fargo nodded.

Miles Stanford sat back in his chair and pressed his fingertips together. "Some things about Carter's actions surprise me," he said blandly.

"Is that so?" Fargo returned, his face expressionless.

"It's most unusual for a general to turn over his command to a junior officer after the battle's over and while he's still able to command," Miles said.

"Is that so?"

"It's also highly unusual for a man to resign from active duty at the same time. That's usually done later and by appearing before a military board."

"Is that so?" Fargo said.

"Carter's wounds are unusual, too," Miles Stanford went on. "Getting a kneecap shot off in battle is certainly possible. Getting both shot off at the same time seems as if it were done deliberately."

"Is that so?" Fargo said.

"Those the only three words you're using today?" The general frowned and Fargo shrugged. "I could wonder if you're holding things back, maybe a great many things," Miles said.

"You could," Fargo said, his face remaining expressionless. "Sometimes it's best not to know too much."

Miles Stanford let his lips purse for a moment before he smiled. "Perhaps," he agreed and thrust his hand out. "Whatever you did, you did it well, Fargo. But there's nothing new about that, is there." Fargo allowed a small smile as he rose to his feet. He had reached the door when Miles Stanford called out to him. "You come away with anything beside the extra pay?" the general asked.

"One thing," Fargo said and Stanford waited. "There's more than one kind of savage," Fargo said and walked from the office. Alison waited outside on her army mount as she held the reins of the Ovaro and he climbed onto his horse. "It's a week's ride to the stage depot at Arborville. There are closer ones," he said.

"I don't want closer ones," Alison said and he saw the faint smile that touched her lips. "I won't ever forget you, Fargo. I'm going to see that you never forget me."

"Now, this sounds like the kind of assignment I'm going to enjoy," he said.

"You will. I promise," Alison said as she rode off with him. She reached a hand out and took his and brought her horse tight against the side of the Ovaro, her leg against him. Promises take many forms, he smiled to himself.

**LOOKING FORWARD!**
The following is the opening
section from the next novel in the exciting
*Trailsman* series from Signet:

**THE TRAILSMAN #151
CROWHEART'S REVENGE**

*Mojave Desert, 1860 . . .
a hellhole of sizzling heat and madness
where only two things could keep a man alive—
dogged duty . . . or cold-blooded revenge.*

"The answer is still no," Skye Fargo said, his voice icy. He
continued to lean casually against the rough wooden wall
of the colonel's office. But Fargo kept his lake-blue eyes
steady, locked on Colonel Power's steely gaze. A long moment passed. Then the officer glanced down at the top of
his desk. The morning light, filtered through the grimy
cracked windowpane, shone across the colonel's face. A
muscle twitched along his jaw.

Fargo studied him. He'd met the man before, years before, in a fort on the Missouri. And now, a thousand miles
west of there, they stood together again in a small room.

Colonel Darrel Power had changed. Changed a lot. His

weathered cheeks were now deep-pitted and a crevice sliced the forehead between his brows. He was unbowed though, his broad shoulders set square, those of a man used to being obeyed. Tough campaigning and the scrapping life in a frontier fort would harden a man to stone, Fargo thought. Or crush him.

The colonel shifted his weight as he stood behind his desk, looking down at a stack of papers. He shifted them purposefully, his jaw working as he thought. Power glanced up again, locking eyes with Fargo.

"I can make it eight hundred dollars," he snapped. "Eight hundred and expenses."

Fargo shook his head slowly. That was a lot of money in the U.S. Army, where a sergeant drew forty greenbacks every two months.

"It's not the money," Fargo said. "I told you I've got business up in Wyoming Territory. And besides, you're not dealing straight with me. I heard two recruits talking on my way into the fort this morning. I heard there's been some newspaperman about to write how the army still can't run down the Indian renegades. These two shoetails said they'd heard you were in trouble. They'd heard your man is dead. Now, I've been around the military long enough to know that the enlisted men usually have the straight story."

The words hung in the air between them. Dust motes swirled in the shaft of sunlight awash on the wide plank floor. Colonel Power's shoulders sagged for an instant and then he turned about sharply and strode toward a map tacked on the wall.

"General Coop doesn't think the major's dead," the colonel said stiffly. "And orders are to go after him. Bring him in."

Fargo walked over to stand beside the colonel and they

looked at the map together. The stained paper showed the diagonal curve of the Old Spanish Trail arcing across the vast wasteland. A large "X" on the trail marked the location of Fort Desoto, under Colonel Power's command for ten years. To the north were a few scrawls in the midst of wide blank spaces. That was where the major and his company had disappeared.

"Just west of here are the Soda Mountains," the colonel said, tracing the wavy lines with his finger. "It's an easy trail to Broken Oak's Trading Post."

"Broken Oak! Is he still around?" Fargo asked, trying to keep the amazement out of his voice. He remembered Broken Oak, the wiry half-breed trader. "What the hell's he doing out here?"

"Trading," said the colonel with a shrug. Fargo noted the tight fake smile on his face. "They do a helluva business, so I hear. Trade with the fort all the time. If he's an old friend of yours, you might ride over and ask him about it yourself."

"Nice try," Fargo said. "The answer is still no."

The colonel ignored him and turned back to the map.

"Then come the Granite Mountains. Easy pass through there. And then you're right at a dry flat and the mouth of Rio Chingo." He ran his finger up a sinuous line that snaked across the blank paper. "Fort Chingo is at the river-head."

Fargo peered at the map in curiosity.

"Oh, it's not a real river," said the colonel, catching his expression. "It's a dry riverbed. Runs sixty miles or so. That's why they call it Chingo. Means short. Short River, see. And there's waterholes in the riverbed. It's a real easy haul for eight hundred . . ."

"Chingo also means naked," Fargo cut in as he stepped

away from the map. "Like naked rock and naked sand and naked sun broiling down. And as to waterholes. Sure. You could trudge up that river and you might find a wallow full of poison alkali water. Or you might find nothing at all."

"Eight hundred dollars."

"No."

"It's an order."

"I'm not in the army, Colonel. And just why is this major so important to you anyway?"

"General Coop's orders," Power said. "The U.S. Army always stands by its men."

Fargo glanced at the map again, his eyes traveling across the blank white spaces.

"How long has Company F been out there?"

The colonel hesitated.

"The major was sent out to establish Fort Chingo five years ago."

"Five years," Fargo repeated.

The colonel walked to his desk and rifled through the papers. He pulled out a small photograph, glanced at it momentarily, then tossed it toward Fargo.

"There he is."

Fargo picked up the tintype and held it angled against the light. In the brown reflective surface, he saw a man's face. The jaw was square and hard, the brow high and intelligent and his light hair was long and wavy. His nose was hooked or maybe it had been broken. But the eyes were what held his attention. Deep and sunken, the major's eyes gazed out from the photograph with an electric ardor, with a look of challenge and defiance. But they were also hunted, haunted eyes.

Fargo tossed the tintype onto the desk.

"How long since they disappeared?"

Colonel Power strode away from Fargo and stood look-ing out the dusty window, his back to the room.

"Two."

"*Two?* Two *years?* You mean you and the U.S. Army sent a company out to the edge of hell and left them there for *two years* with no supplies? No relief? What the hell's going on?"

Fargo saw the back of the colonel's neck redden above the collar of his shirt.

"Drill," the colonel barked, his back still to Fargo, his voice tight with unexploded rage. "Drill. Mounting and dis-mounting sabre drill. Close order drill. Calls and forma-tion." The colonel whirled about, his eyes dark. The rage built in his voice. "Drill maintains the men in fighting form. It's orders. Keep a hundred miles of trail clear for the set-tlers coming in. Keep the Indians from wreaking havoc. Mop up after the Indian agents cheat the local tribes out of land. Orders. Keep the supply lines open for the forts west. And do all that with a quarter of a regiment, five companies from the 13th Infantry. Do it with bad supplies and guns that misfire. Oh, and by the way, run down some rene-gades. Run down Apache devils who are on the loose. If you can spare a company or two."

The colonel whirled about, his face twitching with fury.

"So, you sent Company F."

Colonel Power clenched his jaw. His shoulders were high and tight.

"Major Conrad requested the post," said Colonel Power, slowly regaining his equilibrium. "And after we first lost contact, I sent orders for him to return. He ignored them. So I sent second orders and a dozen men. They never came back."

"So you left them all out there to fry," Fargo said.

He hesitated to ask the colonel another question which would make it appear he would reconsider the job offer to lead a troop to find the missing men. Or whatever might be left of them. But two years out in the worst desert on earth with no supplies. The enlisted men had been right. Major William Conrad and Company F couldn't still be alive. It was a hopeless mission. Besides, he had to get up to Wyoming. There was another job waiting for him there.

"Why don't you send soldiers?" Fargo asked. "What do you need me for?"

Colonel Powers looked Fargo over.

"Because you're the best," he said simply. "Because the officers I've got here are greenhorns. No experience with hard campaigning in the desert. General Coop gave the order—do what you can to rescue Major Conrad. Hiring the Trailsman is the best I can do."

"Sorry, Colonel," Fargo said. "I've got to get to Wyoming. This is a job for the army."

Fargo turned about and let himself out of the office. Behind him, he heard Colonel Power swear under his breath and then slam something down on the desk.

As he made his way past a desk in the main room, a skinny sergeant glanced up at him curiously. Fargo ignored the gaze and left the building. The low frame barracks clustered together. Beyond them he could see the sharp dry horizon against the sky, already white with morning heat.

Colonel Power was a determined man, Fargo thought as he strode across the dusty parade ground. He'd seen the kind before. Power was determined to fulfill his duty and to try to get Fargo to lead the expedition. The mission was hopeless, Fargo knew. The vast tract south of Death Valley was man-killing land. Even without the band of renegade Indians who had taken refuge among the dry bluffs.

Fargo felt a twitch between his shoulder blades and he glanced behind him. Through the window of the headquarters building, he saw the dark blue form of Colonel Power watching him. Fargo turned and continued across the yard.

Just then, a bugle sounded and men came pouring out of the barracks which lined the yard. Fargo stepped aside and took a place beside a low wood frame building.

The men mustered for roll call, lining up in rows of eight. Each wore a navy blue wool sack coat with a single row of smart brass buttons and a forage cap. Fargo's sharp eyes swept over the men, spotting the expressionless hard faces of the regular troops, the expectant bright eyes of the callow cadets and recent recruits, and the deep lined faces of the handful of old soldiers with rows of faded chevrons on their sleeves from the Mexican war.

A tall first lieutenant, his uniform spic and span, strode forward and snapped his heels together. His bright blond hair, neatly combed, shone in the sun. He was followed by a loping old sergeant.

"Sound off!" the sarge called out. The bugler played again.

"Attention!"

The men snapped into sharp rows, chests out, eyes forward. They were sweating in their dark wool jackets as the morning sun beat down.

Fargo watched for the next half hour as the first lieutenant put the companies through their paces, formed up the guard, announced assigned detail, issued the new passwords, and ordered them through the manual of arms. The lieutenant drove them hard, inspecting the men and assigning one double guard duty for not wearing army-issued socks. At last, the morning drill was over and the men were dismissed. Some moved off in groups while others lingered.

Fargo glanced again toward headquarters. The front door opened and Colonel Power emerged. Several passing officers paused to salute. It was time to get away, Fargo realized. Colonel Power was determined to get what he wanted. And what the colonel wanted was to send Fargo halfway to hell to find a man who might have been dead for two years.

Fargo slipped behind the barracks and headed toward the stable. Just as he turned the corner, Fargo was brought up short. Several soldiers were bringing supplies out of a door and loading them into a wagon. A middle-aged private with a pot belly grunted as he let a heavy burlap sack of grain slide off his shoulders onto the bed of the truck.

The private turned back and scowled as a small slender boy emerged from the doorway, bent almost double under a wooden barrel on his back. The boy stumbled and the barrel pitched sideways, splitting open and spilling waterfalls of yellow cornmeal into the dirt. The boy fell, tumbled into the dust, and rolled to Fargo's feet. The kid looked up, his eyes wide.

Fargo started. The kid's face was grimy and a few wisps of red hair stuck out from beneath his dirty cap. His knickers and jacket fit loosely around his small body. But there was no mistaking what he saw. It was a woman.

Fargo reached down and started to offer his hand, then thought better of it. He smiled down at her for an instant and she started to smile in return, then ducked her head, looking away from him. What the hell was she doing here, Fargo wondered. Probably lovelorn and following some soldier to his outpost. Or else trying to get away from one. Whoever she was, she had her own reasons for disguising herself as a boy.

"Your secret's safe with me," Fargo muttered under his breath.

She shot him a surprised look as she got to her feet, beating the dust out of her clothes and pulling her cap low over her eyes.

"What's going on here?"

Fargo looked up to see the blond first lieutenant standing there, his face red.

"Who's responsible for this?" the officer snapped, pointing to the busted barrel. "These are United States Army supplies! Who's responsible?"

"That mangy kid!" the private said.

"Seize him," the first lieutenant said. "This is a waste of supplies. It's against regulations."

The private grabbed her by the shoulder, shook her hard, and then dragged her toward the wagon. The lieutenant pulled a horsewhip from the holster beside the driver's seat while the private threw her down into the street. The lieutenant stood above her, coiling the whip around his hand.

"My boy, we're going to learn about military discipline," he snarled.

"Lay off the kid," Fargo said.

The two of them looked up, startled.

"What's it to you, stranger?" the private cut in. "This here boy came in looking for work yesterday. And he's been nothing but a lazy, shirking son of a bitch ever since. He needs to learn what the army's all about."

"I said lay off."

The lieutenant raised the whip and suddenly brought it down on her. She cowered and yelped as it snapped across her back, shredding the cloth. The lieutenant barked a cruel laugh and raised the whip again. A crowd of soldiers had gathered around and several were egging on the lieutenant.

Fargo tensed his legs beneath him and sprang toward the two men. He smashed into the lieutenant broadside, and kicked out at the private, bringing him down as well. The three of them hit the ground hard. Fargo rolled on top of the lieutenant and kneed him hard in the gut. The air left him and Fargo followed up with a swift uppercut to the jaw that snapped his head backward.

The private rolled and came to his feet. Fargo turned and saw a boot coming straight at his face. He ducked and the kick glanced off the side of his head, exploding pain alongside his ear. Fargo leapt to his feet as the private staggered backward. His powerful arms delivered a shattering right to the man's jaw and then a swift left. The private dropped to his knees and sank to the ground.

"Halt! Halt!"

Fargo heard the unmistakable click of a rifle. He shook his head to clear it and looked up. A crowd of men encircled them. A soldier stood a few feet away, the long barrel of a Winchester aimed right at his heart. Behind the soldier stood Colonel Power.

"What the hell is going on here?" Power asked.

"This man jumped us," the lieutenant sputtered as he got to his feet. The private sat up, rubbing his jaw, his eyes flashing rage at Fargo. "I was just disciplining that boy over there."

She was still cowering near the wagon, hiding her face beneath the shallow brim of her cap. She was obviously uncomfortable being the center of attention. Fargo wondered again what she was doing in this godforsaken fort.

"These two were ganging up on the boy," Fargo said.

Colonel Power looked Fargo up and down. The soldiers standing around them listened closely.

"I could charge you with assaulting an officer," Power

said thoughtfully. "Assaulting *two* officers. Could put you in the guardhouse until I get a tribunal together. That could take a long time."

"I'm a civilian," Fargo said hotly.

"I'm in charge here," the colonel said. "And you're a troublemaker."

Fargo stood considering his options. He sure as hell couldn't shoot his way out of the fort. And even if he managed to slip away, the colonel would press charges and he'd be a wanted man. Damn it. The colonel could make an issue out of an assault charge. And, out of sheer cussedness, he could keep him locked up as long as he wanted.

"Unless you go to Fort Chingo," the colonel added quietly.

At the colonel's words, the girl started and got to her feet, looking from one to the other of them. The colonel took no notice of her.

"Cash up front," Fargo said. Accepting the job, he realized, was the only way out. "Gold, not greenbacks."

"*After* you return with the major," the colonel said.

"No deal."

"Three months in the clink. To start. Take him."

Two soldiers stepped toward him. Fargo held up his hand and they halted.

"Then I want my pay held in a locked box for my return."

"You don't trust me?" The colonel's brows shot up and the men standing around them shifted uneasily.

"No, I don't."

Colonel Power whirled about and started to leave. Then, as if in an afterthought, he turned back.

"All right. You leave at dawn. Your men will be mustered on the parade ground at 0500 hours, along with supplies." He turned to go.

There was a flurry of motion beside the wagon and the disguised woman hurled herself at Fargo's feet and clutched him around the knees.

"Take me with you," she said, looking up at Fargo. In her eyes was a kind of rare desperation.

The colonel turned back.

"What's this?"

"Sorry," Fargo said to her. He leaned down and disengaged her. "That's tough country out there. Not fit for a . . . a boy."

"Who *is* this kid?" the colonel snapped.

"Came in yesterday," the private said. He stepped toward the woman an seized her arm. "Been a passel of trouble ever since."

She tried to shake him off. The private drew back his arm. He aimed a blow at her but struck the cap, which flew off her head. She grabbed for the cap, but missed it and then she glared defiantly. Her auburn hair glistened in the sun, two thick braids wound over her head.

"What the hell?" the private muttered.

"What's a woman doing here?" the lieutenant sputtered. "This is against regulations! Who's responsible?"

Colonel Power took a step forward and looked down at her. She stepped up to him, chin in the air. Fargo couldn't help but admire her spirit.

"You goddamn idiot," Power said to her. "You're going to get yourself killed, you know. Go along if you want to. Just get out of my fort! I've had enough!"

The colonel left hastily and the crowd of men around them slowly melted away. The lieutenant marched off stiffly and the private skulked toward the barracks, still glowering at Fargo and the woman.

"Thank you for what you did," she said, looking up at Fargo. Her face was streaked with grime and sweat, her hair tangled. But her pale blue eyes were forthright and ringed with long red lashes which glistened in the sun.

"Who are you?" Fargo asked.

"Come on," she said. They walked together to a nearby pump, where she washed up, ignoring Fargo. She removed her jacket to reveal a man's shirt which clung to her slender waist. She rolled up the sleeves and pumped water into the stone trough, leaning over to splash it on her face and neck. The shirt fell open and Fargo glimpsed the curve of one small round breast and a dark nipple. She straightened up, dashing the water from her eyes. Her honey skin was smooth and lovely, her lips and cheeks pink. She quickly loosened her hair and combed it out with her fingers, letting the reddish locks fall around her shoulders. Then she expertly pinned it up again.

"There, that's better," she said at last. She dried her hand on her trousers and offered it to him with a big smile.

"My name's Katie. Katie Conrad."

Fargo shook her small hand, impressed by her self-possession.

"Conrad. Major Conrad's . . ."

"Daughter."

Fargo studied her for a moment. Yes, the determined jaw and the high intelligent brow were the same features he'd noticed in the photograph of Major Conrad. But her eyes were blue, clear, and trusting.

"So, you want to come along to Fort Chingo and rescue him?"

"Exactly."

"No," Fargo said, reluctantly releasing her hand. "Between this fort and that one is the worst territory outside of Hades. I admire your gumption, getting dressed up like a boy and sneaking into this fort. But I'm leading that expedition tomorrow. And it's not fit country for a woman."

"A nice speech, mister," Katie said, one hand on her hip, her eyes narrowing. "But let me just tell you that I'm not taking no for an answer. My father's been out there alone for two years and the U.S. Army hasn't done a damned thing about it. I wrote letters, and I went to Washington, D.C. I even came out here last year and agitated. That's why the colonel and I don't get along so well."

"You must have put the squeeze on General Coop, too."

"I did! Wrote him a hundred letters."

"And let me guess," Fargo went on with a smile. "You finally hustled some newspaper journalist to take up your cause."

She nodded.

"That's what finally got the general's attention," Katie said with a note of triumph. "And if you don't let me go with you tomorrow, I swear I'll follow you every step of the way. On foot if I have to."

Fargo looked down at her, considering. She was damned tough for a young woman. And beautiful, too. His eyes traveled down the long line of her throat to the unbuttoned neckline of her shirt. But the trip wasn't going to be a Sunday picnic by any means.

"Leave it to me," he said at last. "You can't help out there. If your father's alive, I'll bring him back."

"No," Katie said desperately, her face reddening. "You don't understand. I've *got* to go. I have these dreams. I hear him calling me. It's fiery hot and I find him all alone and sick . . . he dies in my arms."

Fargo waited, looking down at her. Tears filled her pale blue eyes. She blinked them back.

"What if he's already dead?" Fargo asked quietly.

"No!" Katie said. "No, I can *feel* that he's still alive. I know it sounds crazy, but I *know* he's out there."

Fargo stood looking at her. She was the kind of woman who would stop at nothing. And she really believed this dream. It was what had driven her to take on the entire U.S. Army, including General Coop. And he didn't doubt for a moment that she'd follow him on foot if he started off.

"Tomorrow at dawn," he said, nodding slowly.

"Thank you!" Katie said, suddenly hugging him, her soft body pressing against his hard, lean muscles. Then she stepped away quickly, her eyes serious. "Thank you for everything. I don't even know your name."

"Fargo. Skye Fargo."

She searched his eyes with deep interest.

"They call you the Trailsman."

"That's right."

"I've heard your reputation. Folks say you can outride, outshoot, outtrack any man in the west. Now I *know* we're going to make it."

They smiled at one another. From a distance, he heard the march of troops as the guard changed. Morning was passing.

"I'd better get my things ready," she said, turning away.

"One knapsack," he warned.

"I'm not bringing my silk dresses!" she said laughingly over her shoulder.

"See you at dawn," he called after her.

In the predawn shadows of the parade ground, nine men stood in a scraggly line alongside a mountain wagon. Fargo jerked open the flap of canvas and looked inside. There were kegs of coffee beans and salt pork alongside boxes of hardtack. The usual grim army issue fare. There would be just enough to get them through the trip, he saw. He turned away and inspected the huge water barrels hanging down beside the wagon. They were sufficient, but barely.

The wagon was hitched to six mules, stringy animals, but they'd make it. The wagon itself had seen better days, too, although a glance underneath told him it was solid enough. He straightened up at the sound of approaching footsteps.

Colonel Power approached, followed by the blond first lieutenant carrying a knapsack.

"Is everything in order?" the colonel asked.

"I don't know yet," Fargo said. He turned away from the wagon and walked down the line of men. He felt their eyes on him as he slowly paraded in front of them. It was a mangy bunch for the most part, a different breed from the smart soldiers he had seen the day before. Their faces were suspicious. They wore pieces of mismatched uniforms. Each man had a rucksack on his back and carried his rifle beside him.

"Atten-hut!" the lieutenant called out.

The men pulled themselves into attention. Fargo continued down the line and stopped in front of a fresh-faced kid with freckles across his nose, standing with his chest out.

"How old are you, son?" Fargo asked him.

"Eight . . . eighteen! Sir!" the kid stuttered.

"Like hell," Fargo muttered and continued up the line. At the end, he stopped in front of a sergeant. The man was an old campaigner, his grizzled cheeks silver-flecked and his eyes tough and hard. A row of chevrons were sewn on his shirt.

"How many enlistments you seen, soldier?" Fargo asked.

"Seven," the man said. His eyes flickered toward Fargo's face, then away.

"Name?"

"Joe Dade. Sergeant. Thirteenth Infantry. Company B."

Fargo turned away. The only one of the bunch who looked useful was this sergeant.

"That's the best you can round up for me?" Fargo asked Colonel Power.

"All fine men," he boomed. "Now, you'd better get going."

"Horses. Mules," Fargo said. "Where are they?"

"Infantry," Power replied. "They'll march it. Over the long haul, a good infantry can go just as fast as the cavalry. You'll see."

"I don't care how fast they can march," Fargo snapped. "I want eleven mules for these men. And a remuda, a second string. And add two more mules to the wagon. Good ones. And a horse for Miss Conrad. A fast one." If they got into bad trouble, Fargo thought, he wanted Katie to have the opportunity for escape.

Power opened his mouth to protest, then thought better of it and relayed the order. In a few minutes, additional mules were brought up from the stables. A soldier arrived with a broken-down hay-burner with a bad sway back.

"I said a *fast* horse," Fargo snapped. The soldier shot a look at the colonel and returned to the stables. He was back a few minutes later with a smart-looking chestnut. Fargo laid his hand on the horse's flank. The mare started and lifted her hooves. The horse would be fast all right. And spirited.

Fargo spotted Katie Conrad heading toward them. She wore a riding skirt, boots, and a leather vest. A wide-brimmed hat hung down her back and in one hand she carried a small leather bag.

"That's *it*?" he asked, looking down at the small bag.

"I travel light," she said, handing it to him.

"How's your riding?" he said with a grin, stowing it in the wagon.

"This mine?" she asked, nodding at the chestnut.

He nodded and Katie patted its nose and immediately swung up onto the horse. The chestnut gave a start and started to rear. Kate expertly pulled its head down low and patted its neck with long strokes. The horse moved nervously, stomping and skittering, then quieted. Fargo felt relieved. Katie kept her head on a horse. He hoped that was a sign of how she'd be on the trail.

"You'd better be off," Colonel Power said. "It's getting late."

Fargo realized the officer was damned eager for them to leave and he wondered why for a fleeting moment. He turned and whistled and the black-and-white Ovaro, which had been standing beside the fence, untethered, cantered toward him. The faithful pinto nickered and playfully nosed his shirt. Fargo mounted. A third horse was being led toward the parade yard and the lieutenant prepared to mount.

"First Lieutenant Martin Pike will be coming with you as the commanding officer," Colonel Power said.

"What commanding officer?" Fargo snapped. "I'm in charge of this expedition."

"Yes, yes, of course," Power put in hastily. "But General Coop would never be satisfied if I sent you off without one of my . . . my best officers."

"Just a moment," Fargo said, looking down at the colonel. The Ovaro shifted beneath him. "Let's get one thing straight. Here and now. *I'm* in charge."

"Absolutely," the colonel said agreeably.

"You hear that, Lieutenant?" Fargo asked. Lieutenant Pike was sitting straight up on his horse, listening.

"Is that an order, sir?" the lieutenant asked the colonel.

"This is an *order*, Lieutenant," Colonel Power said, impatience edging his voice. "A *direct* order. Skye Fargo is in charge of this expedition."

The lieutenant saluted smartly, but did not meet Fargo's gaze. Fargo shrugged.

"Let's go," Fargo said.

Sergeant Dade had lined up the men beside their mules. On his order they mounted. Fargo took the lead, riding beside Katie. Half the men rode just behind them, followed by the two wagons, the lieutenant, and the remainder of the men.

They passed through the wide open wooden gates of Fort Desoto. To the east, needles of brilliant light from the rising sun pierced the scattered cloud wisps in the wide clear sky. From northeast to southwest, the Old Spanish Trail snaked its way across the low greasewood hills.

Fargo turned about in his saddle and looked back at the line of men and mules which followed him. The wooden fort, alone on the wide barren flat, grew smaller in the distance. There was a hard pull ahead, he thought, one of the hardest he'd ever faced.

Fargo, with Katie Conrad riding beside him, turned the Ovaro northward, seeking and then finding the trail that led north and west to Broken Oak's Trading Post and finally to Fort Chingo.

It was only later that Skye Fargo realized he should have suspected something. Should have guessed the colonel was holding out on him in more ways than one. But on that bright morning, his thoughts were on the men and woman he was leading into danger. So, he only noticed it in passing and didn't stop to ask himself why. As they turned northward, Fargo's keen eyes read that the trail to Broken Oak's Trading Post looked as if no one had traveled on it for a long, long time.